The Three Kings of Ybor

Volume 1: Eliza Christie's Vendetta

Written By Rock Kitaro

www.StageInTheSky.com

Copyright 2014

Various photos provided by Jen Poblete
and Brandy Scaglione of Exposition Photography

Eliza Christie is the leader of an underground militia hell-bent on avenging her father's murder. **Braden Pierce** is a gifted syndicate enforcer who will do whatever it takes to execute an order. And **Gavin Hassell** is a young narcissistic private investigator who's tired of following rules and not getting the recognition he deserves. The three outlaws become the stuff of legend while the city becomes their battleground. And in their wake, they leave a long list of bodies, a sunken cruise ship, and a half demolished police department. These are the Three Kings of Ybor.

Warning: The following volume contains graphic violence and plausible profanity.

Table of Contents

Prologue – The American Empire in the 2200s

When some people think of the future, they wishfully think that we'll have flying cars and teleportation devices. While it would be nice if people really thought about and poured money into those problematic inventions, everyone knows that war has always been history's biggest moneymaker. Sure ideas and ambition can drive men to strive for improvement. But in the year 2202, the people who really stand up to make a change…those people fully believed in the idea that fighting solves everything.

As expected, a lot has changed from 2014 to 2202. The United States, once a country built on democracy and progressive freedoms, has turned into a machine controlled by men who have never stepped foot in front of cameras. The ones dancing in front of podiums and delivering manufactured speeches were puppets held by the strings of corporations and military leaders. The renaming of the United States of America to the United Empire of America was a joke. America still remains one of the most influential countries in the world, but the real power comes from private CEOs who act according to their own personal constitutions.

I know what you're thinking. How could we have let this happen? Well several factors have led us to this state. One factor was the inevitable World War IV of 2112. This was the First World War in which most of the battles took place on American soil. Several major cities like Philadelphia, Chicago and Los Angeles were destroyed, scarred and left inhabitable from radioactive contamination. The worst part of the war was that millions died instantly from more than two-dozen nuclear bombings. Those nuclear explosions triggered or altered the natural state of seasons. Summer and spring were now next to non-existent with winter and fall lasting throughout the whole year.

In the wake of those conflicts, only one Lieutenant named Tremaine Rose had the courage and audacity to make his voice known from mess halls to lobbies, and eventually to open plazas and packed stadiums. The verve and brio in his vitriolic speeches not only brought his listeners to tears of passion, but inspired them to act on their anger, to turn their negative feelings as a source of motivation. He attracted a cult following amongst the battered soldiers. These soldiers began to follow suit, spreading his word through pamphlets and encrypted e-mail messages to neighboring military divisions.

Lt. Rose blamed the political leaders for their defeat and weak-kneed willingness to bend over to the foreign forces. More than that, he blamed the civilian element for voting those political leaders in office. He preached that you couldn't trust the general public to make an informed decision absent of emotion and irrationality. When it comes to the vote, he felt they relied too heavily on media outlets that carried their own commercial and lobbying agendas. He felt that the reason why we lost was because we were divided as a nation long before the Global Calamity began to affect us. In the face of thousands of civilians, Lt. Rose took the podium and stressed that democracy has failed them. He claimed that we had become a nation of children refusing to grow into adults.

It started with 5,000 strong when Lt. Rose occupied Atlanta. From there, he convinced Gen. Kendall to entrust the 20,000 under his command and struck a deal with Admiral Couth in Jacksonville, Florida to support him with a strong Navy. Mexico, our nation's main opposition under the guidance of the legendary Pres. Morales, was aware of Rose's actions but commanded his subjects to allow it, believing that another civil war was just what the United States of America needed to completely fade into the memory of an ancient world power with the likes of the Romans and Mongolians.

The relatively brief Civil War of 2115 began in Augusta, Georgia and ended with the abolishment of the United States government. In its stead, the American Empire was established on December 1st of the year 2116. Pres. Morales's plan backfired because as it turns out, Lt. Rose, who later became the first Imperial Leader or Provisional Emperor, was well-received by the nation in rallying everyone together for a crucial period of reconstruction. At the time, the people were accepting of a leader who called himself a "dark evil son of a bitch" and lived up to it if that's what it took to make the world recognize his authority.

He forced prisoners to provide slave manual labor, constructing great walls and clearing out the rubble from bombed cities along the Southeast. Heeding the advice of scientists and economic forecasters, he reestablished ties with Japan and Mediterranean nations, providing them with our unused nuclear rods in exchange for new credit, an enormous supply of firearms and upgraded technology.

With the earth a much colder place, instead of Mexicans hopping the border to come to America, Americans were once struggling to find better lives in Mexico. Mexico became one of the world's leading superpowers after establishing the republic entity called the United Nations of Central America.

When the UNCA reneged on their treaty and tried to invade our country again, Emperor Rose saw it coming and put up a better fight with fewer men, using guerrilla warfare and his own brand of terrorism to diminish their ambition that was fueled only by greed and momentum from their prior victories.

For nearly two decades, Emperor Rose was our very own Octavian Augustus. He tailored a new constitution out of the old model with only a few slight modifications. His name was cheered not only throughout the American Empire, but also through parts of Europe and Russia for negotiating a non-violent annexation of the Canadian territories into the Empire and migrating the people out of the cold from the north to the south. Needless to say, parts of the Northern hemisphere were deemed uninhabitable by the Department of Health as places like New York were experiencing an average climate of below thirty degrees year round.

By 2166, Tampa Bay became the largest most populated metropolis in the nation. With the influx of northern civilians, came the competition for underworld power between mob bosses and cartel leaders. While there were good decent people were trying to make new lives for themselves, they had to contend with terror every day from incidents involving automatic gunfire from rival gangs and domestic terrorism.

In 2177, the elected Provisional Emperor of the American Empire had no choice but to amend the fourth amendment of the constitution. Guns were now outlawed to civilians, and even law enforcement had to deal with the standardized high prices of ammunition that became economically comparable to jewelry. Instead, civilians were allowed to carry short-ranged weapons ranging from various sword styles to tasers, nightsticks and extendible pole staffs, concealed or not. The days of people dying with the simple pull of a trigger were supposed to be over. It wasn't.

The gun trade skyrocketed in the underground market comparable to the rise of alcohol in the prohibition era. Weapons were being smuggled off of military bases or sold under the table from generals and lieutenants to the highest bidder. The first man to jump at and seize this opportunity was an ambitious entrepreneur of cybernetics named Isaac Pierce.

By 2184, Isaac used his brothers to manage the gun trade while legally partnering up and selling shares of his patents for mass production with already well-established multimillion-dollar corporations. Overtime, he used his various connections in the underworld to take over those corporations like it was all a chess game, forging alliances with foreign partners and branching off into other subsidiaries, namely, the world-renowned Piece Luxury Hotels.

When the Pierce Corp was founded, this officially launched him into the spotlight as a conglomerate mogul and one of the world's leading pioneers in mechanics, artificial intelligence, and cybernetic organisms. While, in the shadows, he used gangs and Mafioso to carry out hits, heists and acts of intimidation that benefited his corporate agenda, like stock market manipulation and investors suddenly refusing to say no. By January of 2200, Isaac had established the world's first global syndicate by not only unifying the Tampa's crime families under his umbrella, but nearly every governmental entity in the nation had the breath of Pierce upon them.

Timid talks began to surface about the existence of a world-gripping syndicate. It was on the tip of everyone's tongue and made complete sense like the moon affecting the tides. But with no evidence against the world's most prolific employer, the Pierce were untouchable. Isaac was a cordial man, very likable with a contagious smile. He had a lean skinny frame, was of African-American descent and spoke with a proper eloquent tone. So how could this black, seemingly placid man control a world full of ruthless killers and greedy backstabbers? The answer is simple. It's the same reason why the United States became the only super power after the Cold War. He had in his possession a weapon that made the battle for supremacy an a-symmetrical war against all odds.

Chapter 1 – The Jaguar in a School Girl's Uniform

It was a hair-raising fifty-eight degrees on that late August night, but the blood rushing under her neck and shoulders raised her body temperature well above average. The smudged streaks in her thick black eyeliner showed that she had been crying for hours.

Even though she was alone on the train her eyes glared straight forward as if she were staring the devil right in the face. It was enough to make even the most serial rapist think twice because she didn't blink. She just sat there brooding with an intense yet suppressed rage, sporadically clenching her teeth and letting out deep strained breaths from her nostrils.

She wasn't wearing a purse. Didn't carry a cell phone. The only jewelry she had on was a silver heart designed bracelet, one of dozens she owned. With a natural tan complexion, the girl had short curly blond hair with long bangs that scarcely veiled those large emerald green eyes. The blue and gray schoolgirl uniform had her skirt coming up just above her kneecaps with long navy tube socks covering up the rest.

As she sat in the back of the cabin, her hands were wrapped a small foot long Spanish rapier in her laps. She held it as though it were all she had left in the world. As though the future didn't matter. As though everything relied upon it. It was 10:58 on a school night so she was the only passenger riding the last scheduled stop.

The Tampa Bay Rail Transportation Service, affectionately known as the Halo, lit up the city as it did every night. Declared one of the world's new modern wonders, the transit system was a massive ten-lane overpass bridge of railroads that were lifted by columns and suspension cables nearly four stories above the streets below. Rows of solar powered soft yellow LED bulbs were attached under the bridge, set to light up at nightfall.

It was created and designed to provide transportation for the massive influx of workers who migrated from the north. The Halo circled around the entire bay, making any district assessable by rail and spreading the wealth to rural, less developed areas. To cargo ships closing in on the city from the Gulf of Mexico, it really did look like the city was an angel with the large golden ring hovering above. A popular landmark, nonetheless.

The top of the Halo was wide enough to allow passage to eight trains at any given point. There were a variety of different types of trains, from shuttles where passengers stood holding onto handle bars, to seated cabins with wide scenic windows to show off the impressive skyline to tourists. There were both high-speed bullet trains and slow moving doublewide luxurious cabins. And there were a series of well-planned junctions throughout the rail lines that allowed trains to move from the middle to outer lanes with ease. In every town and district, there were dips in the rail lines that allowed trains to descend toward a Halo station for passengers to embark or disembark the train.

This particular cabin that our solitary student was riding in dipped down through a groove in the bridge and came to a complete stop at the Channelside Station in downtown Tampa. It was one of the largest and cleanest Halo Stations with more money poured into advertising on the walls and billboards for tourist purposes. Helpful humanoid androids modeled after real blondes and brunettes stood at every corner of every hallway, ready to answer any questions from commuters. As with the color and theme of the company that owned the Halo line, every android wore the same orange and white uniform that consisted of long skirts, a tucked in blouse and a short jacket.

A voice chimed in through the intercom speakers of the cabin. The elderly woman watching her through security monitor had a motherly tone in her voice. "Here we are, sweetheart. Isn't it a little late for you to be out here this time of night? I wouldn't mind calling you a taxi. I'll even pay your fare."

Eliza's glossy eyes rolled to look out a window. After a hard sniffle, she stood up abruptly and began walking down the center aisle toward the exit.

"No, thank you. I'll be fine." She assured her supervisor in a low grumbling utterance.

Then…For nearly two hours the bold teenage girl traversed northeast from the clean and flashy Channel District of downtown Tampa, to the old brick brewery and cigar factories of Ybor City. This was the historical part of downtown Tampa known for its collection of strip clubs, dive bars, and concert halls. Those old breweries and cigar factories were turned into popular hangouts for the gangs and bikers.

This was where elaborate festivals like the Gasparilla Parade, the Trash Party, and memorial events were held during the day. But around midnight, especially on a weekday, you wouldn't find brave daring high schoolers or even drunk party-hungry college students on the prowl. They would've carried their appetite back to whichever campus or district they came from. There's an urban legend that says at least three people are murdered every night in Ybor City. That legend may have had some legs to stand on.

But there she was, a fifteen-year-old trudging aimlessly along the wide neon lit sidewalks of 4th Street amongst the sultry scene of prostitutes both high class and slutty. The supervising pimps and low level enforcers that assisted him were never too far from their merchandise. The drug addicts didn't look like druggies thanks to modern medical advances that eliminated certain side effects. And as expected and granted by law, everyone carried some type of sword, knife, or nightstick attached to their waists or backs. The more intimidating and jagged the design of the blade, the more the carrier was asking for trouble.

And it was hard to judge who was more dangerous than the other. Some say the ones with the largest most destructive weapons were the worst. Others say the ones with concealed blades were the ones to avoid. Nevertheless, everyone scrutinized her. But the mysterious nature surrounding her presence and the obvious flare of malice that smudged her mascara were enough to make them want to keep their distance.

Helicopters and police sirens seemed to come and go in intervals. The stench of alcohol, motor oil and cannabis was strong even though there was no wind. Through the cloud of music played from the myriad of strip clubs, bars and dance halls, there were screams. Somewhere in the alleys, in the shadows of Ybor, people were getting raped. People were getting hurt. But no one seemed to mind. That's just the way it is.

She even caught a gang of fifteen plaid wearing bikers who were all older then forty, gang banging two blondes who couldn't have been that much older than her. Their hands were scraping against the brick walls at the grown bearded men had their way with them. One of the girls even caught sight of Eliza. The helplessness and misery was tainted in the wells of those blue eyes. But Eliza kept walking.

There was a cop pulled up at a corner talking to two of Barriera's men. Richard Barreira was the mob boss whose family controlled the Ybor district, so it wasn't surprising to see his well-dressed men paying the cops off in full view and blatantly in front of CCTV cameras. The cops stopped counting their wads of cash to examine Eliza like a vulture examining a carcass. And like a diamondback without a rattle, Eliza stared back at the cops without any fear of repercussion. She minded her own business. They minded theirs.

"Isn't it past your bed time honey? Lookin like jail bait with that tight ass!" Said an unsightly woman in fishnets.

Eliza said nothing but kept walking.

She passed by a group of black men in dreads, all wearing heavy sweats and passing around several blunts of rolled cigaweeds. They were standing in front of car trunk speakers that blared gangsta rap. That being said, they showed no shame in ogling her swaying hips as she walked by unfazed.

"Yo yo yo! If that ain't a grapefruit worth squeezing, I don't know what is!" One of them said in the comfort of his homies.

Eliza kept her brooding gaze faced forward. She had to focus on controlling her breaths so as to not appear nervous or anxious. She kept up this act until she reached a bar called "The Dark Oaks". It was the first floor joint of a four-story historical brick building. The top floors acted as a hotel brothel for which local pimps paid a percentage of their earnings to a mob underboss. Purple fluorescent lighting and a mellow blend of guitar riffs emanated from the front entrance. A bouncer twice her size stopped her from entering until she held up a twenty-dollar bill.

"What else?" The heavy bouncer said, unimpressed.

Eliza returned his gaze with an apathetic glance of her own. She then held up her sword and unsheathed the blade a third of the way. The bouncer knew a sharp razor when he saw one. Most carriers wielded swords with dull edges for fear of accidentally killing someone and having a bigger problem than a minor skirmish on their hands. Those who carried blades with sharp edges weren't ones to be tempted. Not to mention it was a light night, and the laid back patrons already inside didn't seem like they'd cause trouble. Thus, the bouncer moved out of her way.

Immediately upon entry the thick aroma of smoke and staunch alcohol threw slightly threw Eliza off guard. It was busy but not packed. It was too early for people to be falling over drunk, but never too early for men to get laid. Nervousness began to set in and break through her exuding air of dominance, but she managed to keep her composure.

The Dark Oaks was a popular hang out for a particular Cuban motorcycle club. A blond, green-eyed teenager entering the hang out sprung about confusion, more so than hostility from an intrusion. To the regular patrons, it must have been amusing to watch Eliza strut from the lobby to take a seat at a table in the center of the room not far from the three-man band. A dark-haired woman in revealing leather straps was warming up in her tease routine in front of the backlight of a large clerestory window. In some sense, the men felt admiration for Eliza's willingness to make herself at home. Most had already made up their minds to leave her alone by the time she laid her rapier on the table with a hard dragging metallic thud.

A Dominican waitress wearing a black shoulder-baring top approached Eliza in stiletto boots. With her eyebrows raised in natural skepticism, she asked. "What are you havin, baby?"

Eliza looked around with caution, her chin low, her eyelids half close. A poker game was in progress at the table next over. The six Cuban men seated all wore a thick padded trinity cross woven in their cuts. The largest, most intimidating of those players was a man named Esteban. In his early forties, Esteban had long black hair and a leathery wrinkled face that suggested he spent too much time in the sun and south of the cold northern hemisphere.

"I'll have what he's having." Eliza told the waitress in an articulate projecting tone. Hers was the natural fiery voice that women attained from shouting their way through countless debates. The kind of voice some women used to terrorize their way out of doing something they didn't want to do. The waitress watched and wasn't fooled as Eliza threw a seductive grin Esteban's way. Esteban was flattered, but it was his companions who all gave the smirked that he held back from showing.

"Little miss prissy? Why you lookin for trouble? These men will come at you like a pack of dogs and toss you all over the place/" The waitress said loud enough for only her to hear.

Keeping her eyes on Esteban, Eliza held up a twenty between her index and middle finger. Insulted, the waitress instantly abandoned her concerned as she snatched up the twenty and walked away. The quick jerk of the bill leaving her grasp caught her slightly off guard. It took a deal of restraint to keep Eliza from throwing a glance over her shoulder at the abrasive waitress.

"Hey buddy, this is our booth. We're here every night. Take a hike!"

Eliza's attention was pulled to a thick agitated voice on the 2nd floor mezzanine. A group of hairy intimidating truckers in black flannel hovered over a young man in a booth. The young man was slouching in a drunken mess, projecting the apathetic aura of someone who was deep in suicidal thoughts. But despite his lack of care and worthless demeanor, something about him struck Eliza's fancy.

"What are you fuckin deaf? Get your ass up!" Another shouted.

Seemingly inebriated, the young man struggled to raise himself from the booth with only his scabbard sheathed Scottish claymore sword in hand. Standing upright, the young man surprised the truckers by towering an inch or two taller than the tallest. Furthermore, some were threatened by the impressive length and size of his sword. Even the strongest swordsman would need two hands to wield a sword of that weight. It wasn't meant for minor scrapes. Swords like that were made not only to penetrate flesh but to crush bones and sever limbs. Perturbed by the sight of him, the oldest trucker grabbed him by his collar and shoved him into another unoccupied booth.

Eliza watched as the young man seemed at ease from being manhandled. He pulled himself together and got comfortable as if nothing had happened. He had a youthful appearance with the build of a natural athlete. The booth he occupied was neighboring another clerestory window, so the soft light from a lamppost shined on the milky white of his smooth cheeks and collarbone. And as he pulled back the bangs of his long greasy black hair that came a little past his shoulders, Eliza was taken aback by the magnitude of his beauty.

The mysterious stranger had thin black eyebrows, long thick eyelashes and a slightly slanted gaze. The irises of his clear royal blue eyes seemed to glow like jewels on display. To Eliza, he was hands down the most beautiful man she had ever seen. An air of enigma bloomed as to why someone of his caliber would be in a dark shitty bar, instead of the bright lights of a runway or posing for some photos in front of a silk waving backdrop.

A blonde waitress, probably still in college, approached his booth completely ignoring the truckers who were waving her down. She set a new bottle of whiskey and two shot glasses down in front of the beautiful stranger.

"So?" The waitress asked him with a hand on her hips. The young man didn't answer but began pouring himself a shot as if she had already left his table. "Gavin? Are you gonna finally invite me over to your place tonight? Or you gonna leave me hangin? Again?"

Gavin tossed the shot back and kept his head back as he let the glass bounce atop the wooden table. Stretching his reach across the shoulders, he continued to lean back in the booth with a lazy sigh of relief as if he had just pulled a double shift. With her self-esteem sinking, the waitress scoffed before storming off, pissing off the hollering truckers yet again.

Eliza's heart rate increased as she watched Gavin's ocean blue gaze gradually lower from the ceiling to the empty shot glass as though it were telling him a story, his hair freely, softly, falling forward again like thin strands of a curtain. Perhaps sensing that he was being watched, his attention then gravitated down to the first floor at Eliza. She was fixated on him, briefly forgetting what she was even doing there in the first place. After a quick scan of her, Gavin gave another apathetic sigh before pulling his long hair from the front of his face and pouring another shot.

"Man…I'd like to run my tongue between the crease of your ass cheeks." A voice from the poker table said.

Eliza looked over at the bald man with a freshly sewn scar on his cheek. "And I'd like to run the edge of my blade between yours." She responded.

"Watchu doing here girl?" Said another Cuban biker from the table that lacked an accent you'd stereotypically expect. "You know this ain't no place for school girls."

The Dominican waitress returned with a mug of beer. Eliza pondered to herself while examining her beverage. Then she let out a question that sparked interest in all who heard it. "Have any of you ever heard of someone named Braden Pierce?"

Initially stunned, the bald biker let out an involuntary chuckle of shock. "Nope. Never heard of him!"

Eliza smirked. "Well then. Seems you don't have what I need." She said before sampling her first taste of alcohol.

Esteban carried a flush of hearts in his hand with over $400 on the table, yet suddenly, he couldn't take his eyes off of that underage blond jailbait. He felt lust, but more so he felt insulted. To Esteban, girls who came appearing to have a strong front must have been a dime a dozen. But it was the temptation Eliza dangled in front of him that brought up old memories. Memories from his younger, more go-get-em days.

"What do you want with this Braden Pierce?" Esteban asked with his grinding nerve-chilling voice.

"You know him?" Eliza boldly shot back.

"Affiliated." Esteban said.

Eliza scoffed. "Pretty much his bitch then, right? Low level guys. Fucking cattle to be done with whatever pops into his head. And the funny thing is, Braden's about my age. Isn't he?" Eliza said before forcing down what was left of her beer and holding back a grimace from its bitter aftertaste.

One of the bikers was about to stand before Esteban put a hand on the man's shoulder and held him in place. "Ignore her. Look at her. She has the look of piss and vinegar written all over her. Someone done wronged her. She probably one of little Braden's exes, hehehe." He said, inciting a round of laughter from his boys.

Esteban's intuition and accusation caught her off guard. Figuring that she'd gathered all she was gonna get from the bar, she masked her frustrations with a gentle laugh before standing. There was one trick left in play. The whole table watched as Eliza walked towards Esteban and grazed against his chair.

Eliza looked down at him and showed off those pearly whites. "Oh! Sorry." She giggled.

Her scent of sweet strawberries penetrated his nostrils and gripped in his throat. She literally took his breath away. Esteban's eyes locked onto Eliza's rocking hips as that skirt swayed from side to side. She headed toward the back exit and opened the door slowly. After stepping out and sending a cold draft in, she made sure to close the door completely behind her.

In the street alleyway, Eliza's promiscuous front of seduction dropped to release a frustrated grimace of disappointment. Things weren't going exactly as she planned so she stopped for a moment to look up at a clear view of the full moon. Letting the cool air calm her nerves, she closed her eyes, relaxed her shoulders and let out a loud alleviating groan. She had just made a fool out of herself and accomplished nothing. Eliza was aware that she was acting recklessly, but the amount of faith she had in law enforcement to handle her plight was a little less than nothing. In her heart, she truly believed that what she was looking for only she could find and get it. It was the how and when that frustrated her.

Wondering aimlessly across the alleyway, she trudged towards the adjoining building. It was a concrete apartment building, worn down and abandoned. The kind of spot addicts and homeless activists used to squat in. She grabbed the cold rusted door handle of the apartment building and opened it just slightly before stopping. For some reason she felt compelled to look back at the door of the Dark Oaks from whence she just came. Like a bystander watching a tidal wave approaching from a distance, Eliza wondered if the bikers would want to follow her.

Underneath it all, she hated herself for that unnecessary curiosity. Perhaps it was the distraction of danger that she needed to assuage the pain of something else. In any case, after waiting in the same spot for close to five minutes, Eliza was about to head inside. Then she heard a creak. Eliza's eyes darted back to the bar's exit. Her eyes were met with the predatory gaze of someone peeking out into the alleyway. Instantly, her curiosity was answered with fear as she exhaled sharply and hurried into the apartment building. Esteban and his five biker buddies barged out of the bar and gave chase, running after her down the hallway.

Sprinting as fast as she could, Eliza made it to a stairwell and continued up, maneuvering around drunken bar hoppers who were just now making it home. The bikers were in hot pursuit, shoving down anyone in their way. They were all carrying matching machetes by their waist, but at the moment hadn't decided on whether they'd use it or not.

"Why you playing games sweetheart? You know what you want!" Esteban taunted with the laughter of his buddies.

Feeling the burn in her quads, the cold dry air squeezing her throat, Eliza reached the third floor and exited from a door out onto an exterior walkway. Bystanders simply moved closer to the apartment doors to give way to the bikers to chasing her. A number of explanations possibly entered their minds as to why a group of middle aged men who could handle their own against football players, would be chasing a high school girl who looked as if she belonged in a children's movie. But in Ybor, staying out of it seemed to be the safest option for the onlookers.

Hope sprung for the bikers as Eliza was running towards a dead end railing at the end of the walkway. That hope went down the drains when Eliza showed surprising agility to jump on the railing banister and balance herself to stand and reach the ledge for the fourth floor. Clearly it wasn't the first time she's had to flee someone.

"Damn!" One of the bikers let out in disbelief. Two bikers attempted to do the same thing, but struggled to simply raise one foot on the rusty painted railing. Esteban and the rest of the bikers stood back and quickly brainstormed for the fastest route to reach the fourth floor that didn't end in a plunging death.

Up on the fourth floor, Eliza continued to sprint as if they were hot on her tracks. She spotted an open window and decided to crawl through it. Halfway inside, Eliza cautiously looked around before tumbling in. White lights from the streets lamps poured in through the cheap clear windows. Breathing heavily, she picked herself up and pulled the bottom part of her uniform jacket to wipe the sweat from her forehead.

Assuming that she was far from safe, Eliza contemplated just picking a good hiding spot and waiting till morning. The room she entered seemed to be an abandoned office space used to store outdated computer monitors and molding wooden desks. The equipment was organized like a functioning office bullpen as if the previous inhabitants left town in a hurry.

Eliza walked down the middle aisle of the office space, scanning the rows for any sign of movement. An eerie feeling crept up on her, prompting her to slowly draw the thin blade of her Spanish rapier from its ceramic sheath. Covering her tracks, she turned around and walked backwards toward a glass exit door at the end of the aisle. When she was within inches of the door, she slowly turned around and reached for the knob. That's when Esteban appeared, slamming into the door's glass panel and intentionally barking like a rabid dog.

Eliza let out a sharp and brief shriek of a scream. With desperation and suspense, she held up her blade with both hands, the tip aimed at his throat. Esteban and his biker boys casually entered the office space either laughing hysterically or wheezing for air. Esteban particularly was panting heavily with sweat oozing from his forehead.

"You see? I don't get why the ladies do this. Eh? They put up a front like they want to be drilled by a bull. Then they take off when the bull uh…polishes its horns." Esteban said with the type of smile that revealed he was impressed with himself.

"Now come on!" One biker's bark acted as the shot to start the races. All men rushed forward, their hands out reaching for her like she was the last drumstick at the buffet. She swung her sword around wildly, promptly halting their advance. But after briefly exchanging comical glances, all of the men rushed her again, aggressively and easily freeing her of the sword.

Esteban took the lead to manhandle and prop her up on a desk. His comrades stood back drooling at the mouth with anticipation as he mounted her. Some were already unbuckling their belts, anxious for their try. Eliza kicked and bucked with all of her might, but it only served to fuel Esteban's vigor.

"Now don't you worry sweetheart. It'll hurt only this once. But tomorrow, it'll feel much better. I promise." Esteban said as he struggled to pin Eliza's surprisingly strong arms down on the desk.

"Get off of me!" Eliza screamed at the top of her lungs. "Get off!"

"Stop struggling. You're gonna mess around and make me break your little arms, little brat! It's usually best if you just let go. Try and relax!" Esteban said with a wide smile.

Amidst her dread and desperation, something caught Eliza's eye. A shadow moved across the windows with the flashing speed of a possessed ghost. One of bikers saw the movement as well. This particular Cuban biker watched as the shadowy figure moved swift and smoothly across the outside walkway, through the same window Eliza entered, and down the aisle toward him in a matter of seconds. The last thing the man saw was a quick glimmer of light before his head was severed from his body.

Esteban recognized the sound of hacking flesh and immediately stopped. He and the rest of his buddies all turned their attention toward the man who was now missing a head. The body just stood there suspended in motion like a statue. After a brief pause of eerie silence, the body dropped to its knees and finally chest to the floor. The man standing over his body was Eliza's young object of desire from the bar.

Gavin's long black hair was tied to the back, not in a ponytail, but by a rubber band to keep his bangs out of his face. He donned a long dark trench coat over dark shadowy military camo pants and a black crew-neck shirt. In his hands, he wielded the long four-foot blade of his double-edge claymore sword. A trail of blood ran through the middle groove of the sword all the way down to the razor sharp tip.

Outraged, Esteban let out a loud war cry before getting off Eliza and hobbling towards Gavin with his machete. Gavin effortlessly dodged a few wild and careless swings before dishing out a swift punch to smash Esteban's nose. As Esteban tumbled backward, holding his nose, his eyes beginning to swell, the four remaining bikers all rushed Gavin with their machetes in hand.

Eliza hurried to roll off of the desk and onto the floor. Staying low to the ground, she scurried around the wood and aluminum desks as the sounds of fast moving footwork and grunts of pain and strength rattled out. Taking refuge under a corner cubicle desk she watched in awe as Gavin, who seemed barely out of high school, take on the big scary bikers with a skill and ease as if he had been battling for generations.

Gavin's speed and precision was a fearsome sight. It seemed unreal. But what was even more surreal was that Eliza didn't pick up any trace of emotion from him. His face didn't show signs of a struggle, anger, desperation, or heroism. Gavin looked more bored and annoyed than anything else. Not knowing why the mysterious young man had stepped in to help her, Eliza was tempted to use the opportunity to take off and run. But just as the thought of escape entered her mind, she saw her small Spanish rapier…just lying there on the ground where she dropped it.

In less than a minute, Gavin had entered the room and cut down the five Cubans without breaking a sweat. All that was left was Esteban. He was just now beginning to stand with a stream of blood and snot oozing down his nose. After taking in the horrid sight of his dead comrades who have spent decades riding by his side, Esteban let out a bellowing cry as he raised his machete and charged towards Gavin. Before he could come close to bringing down the edge of the blade, Eliza emerged from behind a desk and drove her sword through the spine in Esteban's lower back.

Gavin stood in place stunned by this turn of events, but hardly showed it. He merely raised one of his eyebrows ever so slightly at the sight of Esteban's twisted cringes and erratic eye rolls. With burning, agonizing pain spreading throughout his body, Esteban struggled to find the words to say but failed to find them before his soul was gone. Gavin watched with an air of melancholy as Esteban's body dropped to the floor before him. Then he slowly raised his gaze to focus on the blonde girl in a high school uniform.

Her pink eyes were wide opened and jerked as they moved. Her sweat-glossed cheeks quivered uncontrollably and her breathing strained with each exhale. She was in shock, surprised by the thick density of Esteban's body and the amount of strength she had to apply to sink the steel. She had always assumed that due to a sword's sharpness, stabbing someone would by easy for even a toddler. But it wasn't. Eliza had never killed anyone before. She would never forget the jerking tugs she felt as the blade went in and out.

Suddenly…she let out a sad whimper that sounded more like a choking gulp. The whimper gave way to a steady flow of tears and the soft high-pitch cry of helplessness.

Gavin noticed as Eliza's teary eyes shifted from Esteban's body to the bloody sword that was vibrating in her trembling hands. He cautiously raised his huge sword and returned it to the scabbard that was strapped across his back. Then he stepped forward ever so softly as if he were carrying a pitcher of water filled to the brim. God knows where her mental state was, and he didn't want to do anything that would provoke her into hurting him or herself.

Finally showing an ounce of human sentiment, Gavin's morose stillness seemed to suggest he harbored his own share of tragedies. But in his deep blue eyes, he showed more than simple concern for the young woman. He showed a subtle spark of hope. A belief of potential that he saw in her. He slowly reached out to both hands around her wrists and applied pressure to put them at rest. Eliza dropped the sword with a metal chiming thud before looking up to man. As soon as her green eyes locked with his, fear and dread began to subside.

"Tell me your name." Gavin said in a low whispering tone.

"Eliza…" She answered, matching his tone. "What's your name?" She asked him back.

Gavin averted his gaze, as if he were contemplating on whether he should tell her or not. When he stepped over Esteban's body and headed for the exit, he held up one hand and beckoned her to follow. He whispered softly, "My name is Gavin."

Chapter 2 – The Furyx Gene

It was a little half past three in the morning near Cyrus Green Park of the College Hills district, a residential area just north of Ybor. Things were starting to simmer down from the dangerous pace it usually ran. The homeless, addicts, and gangsters had moved their operations indoors by then due to the frigid cold. Gavin and Eliza walked the sidewalks of the brownstone town home and apartment buildings with only a few scare taxis running their routine routes.

Gavin seemed right at home on the placid, yet eerie streets. Eliza followed closely, thoroughly examining him with the curiosity of a step-child with a new guardian. To her, it seemed like Gavin must have spent a great deal of his time alone and by himself. He didn't seem nervous or scared. He just seemed like he was bored with his life, as if he'd have no problem being locked up in solitary confinement for years. He'd probably prefer it.

A single train that transported the Halo's overnight clean-up crew could be heard speeding on the bridge directly above them. The soft orange tungsten light from the overpass gave the couple a thin layer of soft golden tint. Gavin lit up an electronic blue-tipped cigarette. After inhaling deep and exhaling through his nose, he looked over his shoulders at Eliza. He stood at 6'3 but Eliza was tall enough to tilt her head up and kiss his shoulders if she wanted to.

She smiled at him with a deep beam of admiration, while Gavin wore the look of a man who was deciding what to do with a stray kitten. From his examination, he assumed that she was predictable. Just another foolish girl taking chances with her life as if she has nine to spare. He faced forward and took in another puff, again exhaling with agitation. Eliza rolled her eyes, slightly annoyed by his lack of affection. But like a wave coming to shore and receding back, her annoyance faded and a smile returned.

The couple came to a massive four-story brick tenement that was close to the Halo overpass. Gavin entered a numerical code into a keypad and escorted Eliza into Lampel Apartment Place. They could've taken the elevators, but Gavin instinctually preferred to walk the road less traveled. He moved on toward the stairwell in the dusty lobby. The wall lamps were covered in old spider webs and remnants of dead mosquitoes and gnats. The stairwell was lit ever so dimly. The sound from the creaking stairs was unsettling and the smell of wet molding wood filled the air.

Halfway past the third floor and heading to the fourth, a sudden thought of concern grasped Eliza. She concluded that Gavin was slightly strange, give or take. But other than his name and the fact that he was young, Eliza noticed that Gavin didn't ask any questions. Gavin was a murderer. And by the way he handled himself, it may not have been the first time he's brought death with him.

"Are you going to rape me?" Eliza asked all of the sudden.

Gavin stopped in his tracks, turning and looking down at her with a subtly look of absurdity. Perhaps thinking of the most appropriate response, the most he could come up with was, "Do you want me to?"

Eliza pondered to herself briefly. Then just like that, abandoning all thoughts of concern, she looked up with a promiscuous smile and said, "Yes."

There was an awkward pause with the two of them standing in silence on the stairway. Then, Gavin scoffed with the first smile she'd seen from him. They continued up the stairwell.

On the fourth floor, Gavin's apartment was the fifth door at the end of the hall next to an access door that would lead to the roof. Gavin's home was a neat and clean wood-floored one-bedroom studio with a clear skylight that conveniently showed the full moon in the sky. Other than the moonlight, the only other source of illumination came from a tall lamp in the far corner of the room near the kitchen. It was meagerly furnished with no decorations, no TV, only a couch set, a dining table with one chair and a twin size bed by a window all in one room.

Eliza removed her uniform jacket and sat down on the recliner. The heater working at full capacity made her feel at ease as she clasped her fingers above her head and reached to the roof to stretch her back. Loosening the top three buttons of her white shirt, she watched as Gavin went through his usual routine of coming home from a long day.

Gavin placed his sheathed sword down on his neatly folded bed before taking off his trench coat and hanging it up in the closet. Eliza's heart started to beat faster as Gavin removed his solid black shirt, revealing a lean muscular physique that lacked any blemish or discoloring. After folding the shirt and putting it in a dirty hamper, Gavin went to the sink counter that was positioned outside the bathroom door. He threw on some water from the faucet and while drying his face with a hand towel, he could see Eliza's reflection in the mirror.

She was watching him with a seductive smile that said it wasn't her first time alone with a male. Her arms were spread back like a butterfly on the recliner's shoulders. The soft yellow glow from the lamp created an aura around her already rich healthy blond hair. Her legs were crossed, showing off the well-toned thighs half covered by her skirt. Gavin squinted his eyes, still trying to figure her out. Not to mention he didn't exactly find her stench of sweat and ruined eyeliner all too appealing.

"How old are you?" Eliza asked in a cute and playful tone.

Gavin stood up straight and turned around to face her. "Nineteen." He answered plainly.

Reaching into his closet he found a black tank and put it on. Eliza snickered to herself as Gavin walked over and sat down on the sofa across from her. Eliza already deduced that he was androgynous from the neck up, but she found it narcissistic the way he constantly pulled his hair back and tucked it behind his ears. Aside from his impressive physique and height, if one were just to look at his face, nobody would raise an eyebrow if you'd mistaken Gavin for a female model. Eliza didn't feel silly about it. In the bar she did. But in his apartment with the man sitting just ten feet away from her, she believed Gavin's beauty would even put hers to the test. Settling in, he lit an e-cigarette and sighed deeply as he put an arm over the sofa's headrest and stretched out his legs.

"Aren't you gonna ask me how old I am?" Eliza asked.

"Too young. Which means it doesn't matter." Gavin spoke in a low monotonous tone that was naturally only loud enough for his intended audience to hear. Eliza also found it quirky and cute how each word he uttered seemed to be a burden to him, as if he subconsciously thought his words were a waste of time to say.

"That's weird. You don't exactly strike me as a law-abiding citizen. Are you on the way to the army?" Eliza asked.

Gavin thought the question was out of the blue. She picked up on his quick glance of perplexity and threw a point toward the large duffel bag leaning neatly against a corner in the room. Gavin scoffed with a slight smirk and answered, "Marines. Just got out."

"Oh!" Eliza said as she kept nodding her head with a chipper smile.

The unwavering schoolgirl act was starting to annoy Gavin. "Are you thirsty or something?" Gavin asked before blowing smoke out of his nose.

Eliza slowly pulled herself up and moved to sit on the couch closer to Gavin. "You know what I'm thirsty for." She whispered before biting down on her lower lip.

Whilst kneeling on the couch Eliza leaned forward, chest over Gavin, and moved in for a kiss. And just when she was so close as to feel the breath from his nose upon her lips, her affections were met with a dramatic, mood-killing…"What's with you?"

Eliza recoiled back and scoffed deeply from the pit of her throat. "What?" She asked with a surfacing scowl.

Casually rolling his eyes in a fashion that ended with one of his thin eyebrows raised high, Gavin let out an agitate sigh. "Hours ago, you were ready to die. Now you're ready to lose your virginity to a man you barely know. Self-destructive…Must have a reason." Gavin said as if he were speaking aloud, primarily to himself.

Deeply offended, Eliza impulsively slapped Gavin across the face sending the cigarette flying and leaving an imprint on his face. His own temper rising, Gavin took hold of her upper arm and shoved Eliza backwards into the recliner with such momentum that it nearly sent the chair tumbling backwards. Eliza was stunned. He shoved her with ease as if he were tossing a stuffed animal. Before she could continue to ponder over what just happened, Gavin quickly shot up to stand over her with a look of disappointment, like a mentor to a pupil. Initially defiant from his aggression, Eliza began pouting heavily and broke down into tears.

"I'm sorry! You're right. I just don't know what to do." Eliza whimpered as she covered her mouth.

As any man would feel, Gavin's heart gradually softened at the sight of the tears. He approached to her knees and squatted down to her level. "What happened? Tell me." He said in a tone that, for the first time, showed some sense of genuine concern.

As Eliza looked into his crystal clear blue eyes, the tears in her own glossy green eyes began to sting. The guilt and shame put a lump in her throat but she struggled to convey, regardless. "I...My dad... My father was killed last week by this contract killer named Braden. I know his name because it was the last thing my father said. It wasn't my name! It wasn't leave my daughter alone! It was Braden. And he butchered my father with a sword. He killed him right in front of me."

Gavin nodded. "You think this Braden is connected to *the* Pierce? As in the Pierce Corporation? The syndicate? That's why you were asking about him to some random gangsters in a shady bar?" He questioned.

Eliza nodded before bringing in her legs to her chest and wrapping her arms around them. Gavin stood up and casually returned to his sofa. He scoffed at the ridiculousness of her plan and plopped down in his seat.

"Twas very foolish I think. Damn near every family and gang out there on the streets and around the world full under the shadow that the Pierce cast. They have political connections, fire power, entire law enforcement agencies on their payroll. They own banks, casinos, hotels. They are the arch prototype of a well-oiled organized crime machine is supposed to be. Hence, they're called a syndicate." Gavin said casually in a tone that had a thin tint of mockery.

Half a minute went by with Eliza just sitting there astounded by Gavin's sharp criticism. She slowly looked up at him with a vindictive eye-squinting scowl. "Foolish? Yah think? Or is it, you say that cause you just don't know?" Eliza asked.

"Cause how could you know? Huh? To walk into a room and see some punkass thug who should be out there boosting cars, standing over the only family member you had left in this fucked up world. How could you possibly know how that feels, Gavin?"

Eliza's voice grew louder and angrier. Soon, she was standing tall on her two feet. She began shouting as if she was talking to herself in an empty room. Her fists were balled and she accentuated the last word of every sentence.

"Who the hell does he think he is? That punk bitch! And foolish you say? What's foolish is that rat-faced bastard thinking he can get away with it! That's what's foolish! Cause I'll tell you something else! I don't care if he's the godfather himself? I'll bite out his black heart without a twitch of the eye. I'll strangle him and force a blade down his closed throat. I don't care! And I'll find him! Anyone who gets in my way will just be road kill. I WILL MASSACRE ALL OF THEM!"

Suddenly, the Halo's maintenance line sped by on the bridge outside the window. The sound of it startled Gavin as if a bullhorn went off right by his ear. To Eliza, the enhanced silencing technology of the train's wheels was barely audible. She heard it, but to her, it wasn't so loud as to make anyone jump the way he did. It was more like a soft whistle from a tea kettle.

Gavin had no idea how completely entranced he was by Eliza's declaration. It left him speechless and took his breath away. Never before had he seen anyone who demanded such entitlement. Was she deranged? Or just plain ignorant? From her speech and the way her cheek quivered with each barking syllable, Gavin was convinced. He was convinced that there was nothing he could say or do to deter her from the ambitiously suicidal and extremely vague mission she hoped to embark on.

Eliza observed as his gaze wandered low, bouncing at various spots on the floor. She knew he was keeping all of his thoughts to himself. And it was infuriating that he wasn't revealing those thoughts after she had just revealed an emotional chapter of her life. Eliza sucked on her teeth before snatching her jacket from the floor. Gavin sat and deliberated, calmly watching the hot-blooded youth whip her arms into the uniform jacket and tuck the small rapier in the belt loop of her skirt.

After buttoning up the top three buttons on her white blouse, she delivered a final scowl of spite towards Gavin and headed for the door. Just as she turned the handle, Gavin stood up from his seat and snapped for her to wait. Eliza slowly stopped with reluctance, not really wanting to hear what else he had to say.

"Sit down." Gavin said bluntly as he massaged his chin, still wondering if his decision was the right one.

Confused yet intrigued, she hesitated to do as he asked. But after a brief stand of defiance, she finally let go of the door handle and sat back down on the recliner. Her face was flushed and she was still pretty steamed. This added with the fact that she was wearing her uniform jacket made her sweat. Refusing to show her discomfort, Eliza simply crossed her legs and raised a single eyebrow, tilting her head at an angle to scratch that eyebrow, mentally telling herself that she was only granting him two more minutes of her time.

Gavin walked over to retrieve his duffle bag from the corner of the room. With care and caution, he slowly placed it on his bed and began shuffling through it. Eliza watched with gradual annoyance, propping her head up with an elbow on the armrest and letting out a mild cough of congestion.

"When I was in the Marines last year...because of my outstanding athletic ability amongst other qualities...I was given the option to join a secret infantry group within the 1st Division GCE, 2nd Battalion, 5th Regiment. The esteemed Raiders. I gratefully accepted." Gavin began.

His words and low volume, deep bass voice held her attention.

"Most civilians don't know, it's kind of on the low down right now. But there's this steroid they give you. Kind of like a performance enhancer. From what I was told, it was developed by a pharmaceutical company exclusively for the military. It sells for hundreds of thousands on the black market. It supposedly gives you the strength of ten men and the speed of two Olympic sprinters. You can hear things from far away; see things like seeing through the eyes of a hawk. And it makes your skin nearly bullet proof." Gavin explained.

He turned to look at her. "Don't get me wrong. If you get hit with a large enough caliber bullet that can penetrate armored plating, you're going down. Your skin still feels like skin, but the muscle beneath it is more dense. But since civilians aren't allowed to carry guns anyway, I wouldn't worry too much about that."

Gavin walked over to Eliza and knelt down. He held up and opened a small palm-sized case that was made of pure chrome. Inside the case was a small clear vial of red liquid that appeared to be blood. Gavin held the vial up to Eliza like it was a valuable gem glistening in the light.

"It's called the Furyx Gene. It's how I followed you tonight. It's why those hardcore wannabe MCs didn't stand a chance. One shot is all it takes and you're set for life. They say only a Furyx user can take down another Furyx user. We're the only one's strong enough to swing a blade powerful enough to penetrate each other's skin." Gavin told her.

Eliza's eyes were just about to widen with excited anticipation before Gavin abruptly stood up with a serious expression. "But there's a catch. We were merely given the option of taking it. If we said yes, the Empire made us sign a liability waiver. You see, there's an extremely high chance of a man suffering from brain hemorrhaging. You can die from it, Eliza. I've seen it."

Gavin's lips lazily began to curl into a lopsided sadistic grin. "And Eliza…I'm telling you. If you take this, the nerve-racking pain you'll feel is unlike anything you've ever felt before. It comes to the point where you really do want to just bash your own head open."

"Then why'd you take it?" Eliza asked with a judgmental tone.

"I knew I could handle it."

Gavin shrugged with a smirk as he tucked some of his long bangs behind his right ear. Then he walked over to the bed, took off his sword and propped it up against the headboard. Setting the duffel bag beside him on the floor, he looked over to Eliza and waved her over to join him. Eliza didn't hesitate. Within minutes Eliza was lying face up on Gavin's bed. Her wrists and ankles were tied by towels to the railings. Gavin was kneeling beside her, attaching a syringe to the top of the Furyx vial.

Eliza watched him and took note of the care he showed in making sure everything was in order. "Gavin. Why are you doing this for me? You could sell this stuff and make a small fortune." She asked.

Gavin sighed with a smile before rubbing the back of his hand against his own forehead. He was finished and ready to insert the needle, but took the time to answer her question. "Eliza. I find you fascinating. In all honesty I just want to see what you can do with it. As far as my finances go, well…What can money get me that I can't get for myself?"

"Mmm…spoken like a true outlaw." Eliza smirked.

"Indeed." Gavin added. "Are you ready?"

Gavin couldn't help smirk at her obvious admiration for him. Her gaze was fixated on his eyes, his hair, and then his lips. Her chest elevated up and down nervously. "Kiss me first." She requested.

Gavin thought the request was an odd one but he was well aware of the effect he had on women. He couldn't blame her for asking if it may be the last request she ever makes. Slowly, the dark mysterious blue-eyed angel moved in and pressed his lip gently on hers. The satisfaction it brought her released a single tear and ushered in a smile that showed a trace of sadness. With last second thoughts slipping in, Gavin turned his heart cold toward the tears and whispered his own request of forgiveness. Having made peace with his decision, he gently tilted her head to the side and stuck the needle into her neck pressing hard on the injection.

The pain hit Eliza like a jolt of electricity. Clenching her teeth, her eyes shot wide open. She let out a loud hair-raising scream as if she had just been stabbed through the back of her thigh. The scream was piercing and carried. Gavin snapped his head toward the door, hoping no one came knocking. For a full twenty minutes Eliza screamed and convulsed in pain and agony before finally blacking out due to exhaustion and shock.

…

The night went and morning came.

…

There was no sign of Gavin. Eliza lay in his bed, sleeping on sheets that were soaked with her own sweat. Suddenly, a silent speeding Halo train ran past her window and Eliza shot up from her slumber, grimacing and struggling to reach her ears.

"Holy shit! What the fuck!?" She screamed as the train continued to pass by. In the struggle, she obliviously managed to rip her left wrist free from the towel and cover one of her ears.

"What the fuck is that?" She shouted as she looked out the window.

Then, she began squinting in agony as if someone was shining a high powered spotlight directly at her face. The light from the sun was blinding. Eliza continued to shoot off a few more f-bombs and use God's name in vain. Eventually, she was able to rip the towel that bound her right wrist and cover her tear swollen eyes with both hands.

Once the trains were gone and all was quiet, she carefully lowered her hands and slowly opened her eyes to look straight ahead. Uncontrollably, her vision began to zoom in and out of the tiny needle-like holes of the brick wall across the room. As if that wasn't enough: exaggerating her irritation, she then began to notice the itching sensation beneath her skin. Her sense of touch was so acute that she could feel the blood racing through her veins. It was irritating, but manageable compared to the bright lights.

Blinking heavily, she scanned the apartment. "Gavin? Gavin, where are you?" Eliza called out.

She managed to spot a napkin on the floor beside her bed. There was a message written on it. She leaned over to pick it up and became further annoyed when she realized that her ankles were still bound.

Wiping the sweat from her forehead, Eliza squinted to read the napkin. It said, "Don't do anything foolish Eliza. I hope you find who you're looking for. –Gavin"

Disappointed, Eliza rolled her eyes before muttering to herself…"Great."

Chapter 3 – For your own good…

After a long night of recklessness and teen rebellion, Eliza was now riding in the passenger seat of a golden luxury sedan. It was a school day but she was dressed in warm traveling clothes under her favorite long light-green hooded overcoat. The coat used to belong to her departed mother, sparking her infatuation with the color green. After the death of her father, custody of Eliza fell into the hands of her father's partner on the force and best friend, Detective Angel Gazi.

Gazi, pronounced gay-zi, was a man in his late thirties. He was of mixed Cuban and Puerto Rican descent. He was tall, with distinct thick eyebrows that were almost as thick as his rich horseshoe shaped mustache. Gazi was a rare breed of detective, the type who wasn't on anyone but the government's payroll. Despite his minimal salary, he always appeared clean in his suit and pants that were always ironed and in pristine condition.

Gazi was beyond pissed at the moment. As he maneuvered in and out between the afternoon rush hour traffic, his mind struggled to filter which words to say to the fifteen-year-old daughter of his old friend.

Eliza knew Gazi well. Ever since she was little, Gazi was the one person who always treated her like an adult. Always asking for her input on crooked cops and how twisted the political situation was in the United Nations of Central Americas. He was the only one in her life who she thought saw her as an equal. And as such, she respected him and felt comfort in the fact that she would be in his custody. But after hearing Gazi's decision in response to her night of going AWOL, her respect for him was dwindling.

Gazi kept throwing quick glances at her while handling the congested traffic. Despite the puzzling fact that she kept blinking in an erratic manner, she wore a constant grimace of spite and discontent. Gazi was unaffected.

"I don't know what to say to you, Elizabeth. Here, I give you a chance with a clean slate. Completely ignoring your stints at what, six different alternative schools? Completely ignoring the rumors about you starting a gang riot in eighth grade. And this is how you repay me? Do you have anything to say for yourself?" Gazi asked in a clear tone that lacked any Hispanic accent.

"Those were all-girl schools. We were all delinquents so it was bound to happen." Eliza scoffed.

"I said, do you have anything to say for yourself girl?" Gazi sternly asked again.

"Would it convince you to change your mind?" Eliza asked.

"Nope." Gazi said bluntly.

"Then what's the point?" Eliza said as she tried to prop her head up by her elbow and ended up accidentally bumping her head on the glass window. This only aggravated her frustration, by which an involuntary bite on her lower lip helped ease some tension.

"Responsibility is the point. Cause and effect. What's going to happen is the effect that you caused. Accepting responsibility is at least a step forward." Gazi responded.

Eliza scoffed as she looked out the window. Responsibility was an attribute Eliza simply could not understand in her state. Cruising west bound on the Interstate, they were approaching the junction with the letters on the signs of the Tampa Bay International Airport gradually coming into focus. Sadness began to overtake her and desperation kicked in. Her eyebrows drooped and the gloom of a girl lost in the forest faded in.

"Gazi, look I'm sorry. I was just overcome with grief. Okay? You don't know what it's like to be in my shoes. To see what I saw. All right? But I got it out of my system. Okay? It won't happen again. Please don't do this. I'm begging you. I'm literally begging you."

Gazi pulled onto the exit that led straight to the airport before taking the time to look at her thoroughly. Eliza showed a puppy dog look of regret and remorse that could sway even the most pious state trooper to hold back on giving her a ticket even if he was behind on quota. But for Gazi, after a long hard look, he let out a blunt, "I ain't buying it."

…

"Well fine then! Fucking pig! I don't fucking need you! I hope you get shot tonight! I hope someone clips your tires and you drive this piece of shit car off the fucking bridge and drown. Dirty ass disgusting spic!" Eliza shouted as she dramatically bounced around in her seat, finishing off the tantrum by folding her arms and turning to look back out her window.

Gazi laughed hysterically, almost in a sadistic manner. "There's the Lizzy I know. Let it all out. Come on, you got more?"

Eliza glared at him with a menacing scowl. "You don't even know the half of it. If I wanted to, I could fuck you up right now." Eliza threatened.

"Yes. Yes. I would love to see that someday." Gazi said as he put on his sunglasses.

"I could! I'm stronger than…like you don't even want to know right now!" She blurted out.

"Alright, alright. Sit back and shut up. And why the hell are you blinking like that?" Gazi asked, finally getting annoyed with it.

"My eyes hurt, alright! Fuck off!"

"That mouth's gonna get you in a lot of trouble one day, Eliza. You need to stop all that goddamn cursing." Gazi said sternly.

"Fuck. Fuck. Fuck. Fuck. Fuck. Fuckity, fuck, fuck, fuck! Do something!" She barked. Gazi simply shook his head. So Eliza followed up with, "Yeah, that's what I fucking thought."

Her anger gradually turned to hopelessness as the frequency of passing airplanes increased. It may have been that hopelessness which aided her in ignoring the pain from the golden rays of the setting sun. Her green eyes were beginning to adjust to the light. Tampa was where she was born and raised. It was the greatest city in the Empire of which she had taken for granted. The thought of leaving behind everything that reminded her of her father was heartbreaking to say the least.

Within the next two hours, Gazi and Eliza went through the rigorous security hoops one had to go through to board an airplane. Obviously there were no weapons allowed in the airport, and all passengers had to wear an electronic bracelet that monitored their heartbeat, alerting authorities if anyone's heart pressure began to spike beyond normal.

Eliza was now sitting in the lobby of her gate, her face planted in her hands crying her eyes out. Feeling some sympathy for her, Gazi shopped at a nearby kiosk looking for some souvenir or toy that might bring her any comfort. After fifteen minutes, all he could come up with was a bottle of orange juice. Eliza accepted it, probably knowing that it may have very well been the best Gazi's socially challenged mind could come up with. He sat down beside her, the both of them waiting on a boarding call.

"Taste good?" Gazi asked.

Eliza didn't answer. She finished her juice and placed the empty recyclable bottle beside her small brown carry-on bag that was made of faux animal hide. After wiping her eyes, she went back to burying her face in her hands again.

Sighing with a heavy heart, he beseeched her. "Elizabeth. You have to understand. I'm doing this for your own good."

"Ah, you're just a coward! Passing on your responsibilities!" Eliza shouted as she slowly raised her head and showed her red flushed face.

However disgusting it was for Gazi to see her face all scrunched up and wet, he more so embarrassed by bystanders who overheard her and cast judgment on him. "Look Eliza. Alright. I know. I know what you're going through. I know you must be-"

"Stop." Eliza said as she stood up and sniffed up her tears. "Stop right there. Alright? Trust me. You have no idea how frustrating it is to hear people say, I know how it feels. Bastards. No, you don't."

Gazi smiled as he leaned back in his seat. "Liz. You need direction."

"Right! So you're shipping me off. Mister… I'mma take care of you, Elizabeth. I'm gonna make sure you're looked after." Eliza mocked before folding her arms. "Please. Fucking joke. I might as well be in foster care."

"My sister is a good woman. She'll take care of you. As much time and attention as I'd like to give you, with my job and the focus it demands…" Gazi sighed before digressing.

He stood up and approached to put his hands on her shoulders. "I didn't want to see you in foster care. I've known you since you took your first steps behind your father's back. Your mother died giving birth to you. You need a good female role model. Especially after that stunt you pulled last night."

Gazi put on a smirk. "You're lucky I don't put a collar around your ankle. That's what my deputies do to their kids."

At long last, an uneasy smile surfaced. Eliza moved closer and planted her face into his chest. Gazi embraced her. "Why doesn't your sister live here?" She complained.

Gazi sighed. "Because her husband's a fugitive." He answered reluctantly.

"Ha! Right. Good role model." Eliza muffled through his shirt.

"Now boarding! Flight 818 to Seoul of the Korean Republic." A call was announced over the PA system as Eliza's plastic electronic boarding card lit up to alert her.

Gazi patted Eliza on the back before freeing himself to grab Eliza's bag. Spiking his eyebrows, his quick head nod asked her if she was ready to board. Eliza nodded before she let Gazi lead her toward the terminal doors.

"Trust me, Elizabeth. My sister is the purest person I've ever known. She's very understanding, and probably knows better than most what it means to follow her heart and leave the past behind."

"Okay?" He said while leaning over to her. Eliza nodded like a toddler as she wiped the tears from her flushed face. Gazi snickered as he gave Eliza one last hug, whispering in her ear, "You'll do fine."

Eliza handed the reception android her boarding card to scan. After taking her bag from Gazi, she waved to him with a sorrowful pout that would tug at any mother's heart strings. The walk down the skyway tunnel toward her plane was comparable to walking the plank. Not knowing what to expect. Not knowing who she'd meet, or how she'd live. There were too many unknowns that lay before her. The only thing she was sure of at the moment was a lonely sentiment. She was leaving the only place she ever called home. There was nothing else.

Chapter 4 – Seoul, Korean Republic

It was late in the afternoon. The sinking sun cast a pink reddish tint on the clouds that one would usually see in the morning. Polite, upbeat announcements from an inviting automated female voice echoed around the high ceilings of Incheon Airport in alternating languages. It was a peaceful serene scene as an eleven-year-old brother and a nine-year-old sister stood with their faces planted against the thick glass window panels. The airplanes taking off and landing on the runway were enough to keep them occupied.

Their mother stood checking the flight listings in front of the large LED arrival/departure board. She was a petite woman in her early thirties, but had a fair light-skinned complexion and a small face that suggested she was in her early twenties. The mixed Latino breed wore a long modest orange dress with a white flower pattern. Her hazel light-brown eyes were complimented by a natural red hue that subtly appeared at the tips of her long dark brown hair.

"Oh! You're already here." Boa said aloud to herself, pleasantly surprised.

A huge jumbo jet the size of a cruise ship was passing by the waiting room and dwarfed the brother and sister gawking at it. Both let out an impressed, "Wow" in unison. The married couple of elderly Korean natives found the siblings adorable and couldn't help but chuckle.

"Cloud! Rain!" Boa called out.

Cloud turned to see his mother waving at him from the hall outside the waiting area. He grabbed his sister by her shoulder, "Come on Rainy."

The children ran to their mother who squatted to greet them with a warm smile. "Did you see the airplanes?"

"Yeah!" The two answered as Boa giggled at the cuteness of their youthful voices.

Cloud and Rain stayed close to their mother's side as she navigated through the richly developed airport that was protected by a strict socialist government. They marveled at the large holographic advertisements that illuminated the walls and island kiosks. They held on to their mother's skinny legs as they rode the terminal shuttles that passed over a large green golf course and Olympic sized swimming pool, just two of the many features hosted by the international friendly airport.

"Mom. Can we live here?" Rain asked her, prompting laughter from Cloud. His laughter was very clear, distinct, and naturally haughty. One that got many bystanders turning their heads his way.

Boa gently caressed the top of her head. "No sweetheart. We already have a home."

"But this place is so much bigger." Rain said with a toothy smile.

"Nah. Too many people." Cloud said in his 2nd language that was Japanese.

Eliza was waiting in the baggage claim area of the arrival lobby. It didn't take long for the gripping sense of self-consciousness to take over. She was the only Caucasian in the room. Everyone else stared marveling at the beauty in her green eyes and vibrant golden blond hair. Eliza instinctively released an uneasy smile as she sighed and covered her head with the hood of her overcoat.

The conveyor belt finally started to bring out the passenger bags when Eliza heard a soft voice behind her. "Um. Elizabeth?"

Eliza did a quick 180 to see Boa standing behind her with a bright smile. Rain gawked at the sight of Eliza who stood nearly an inch taller than her own mother. Eliza was speechless and stunned by Boa's unique beauty that was completely unexpected, given the sight of her older brother.

"It is you, isn't it? Hello! I'm Boa." She greeted warmly with a ninety-degree bow.

Eliza took off her hood and extended her hand to shake Boa's. "Eliza... You're Gazi's sister?" Eliza asked as politely as she could.

"Yes. Are you surprised?" Boa said with a chuckle.

Eliza couldn't contain her smirk. "Ah...I'm sorry. Ha ha! I just don't see the family resemblance." She said, feeling a little ashamed of herself.

"Yes! I was complimented about that a lot when I was little. Speaking of children. This is my daughter, Rain."

Rain gave a shy wave while showing off the gaps between her baby teeth. She chuckled that nonsensical chuckle that simply said she was thrilled. Eliza involuntary leaned back as she waved to the little girl, so far, thoroughly impressed with the welcome wagon.

"And that one behind you is my ever handy son, Cloud." Boa continued.

Eliza turned around to see Cloud rolling over Eliza's two green suitcases. Eliza wondered how he knew that they belonged to her. Cloud observed her obvious bewilderment and answered, "I took a wild guess." He said in a haughty tone while gesturing for Eliza to look at the conveyor belt. Eliza turned and noticed that almost everyone else had the same kind of luggage. Small black roller suitcases.

Half an hour later, Eliza was riding shotgun in Boa's dark purple electronic SUV. It was dusk just before nightfall. The bright lights of the city were beginning to emanate. Korea was just like America. Other than a handful of massive metropolises, other cities and townships looked like third-world villages, full of ruins and battle scarred roads and bridges. Seoul was a metropolis that maintained its advanced civilization and never ceased to grow, much like Tampa Bay.

Eliza looked out the window, taking in her new environment as Boa drove through the busy commercial district of Gangnam. The tall, bright and colorful skyscrapers were just like home to her, except their architecture was more ambitious and strange. The designs seemed to have an aura of danger about them with some buildings donning jagged edges like flames and other buildings playing with spiral curves.

And people… Just like home, the crowd, young and old, traversed the shopping districts like busy ants. Everyone was dressed warm. She noticed the groups of teenagers hanging out by fountains and outside arcades. Everyone was of Korean or Asian descent with only a few white and black girls sprinkled about. But even the foreigners she saw seemed so well assimilated, decked out in accessories of their favorite cartoons with colored hair and light blinking shoes. To Eliza, they all seemed like happy sheeple, blissfully unaware of the dangers of the world. They were all so happy and upbeat. She wondered how she'd ever find a friend amongst them.

Inside the SUV, it was quiet and awkward. Cloud and Rain stared at the back of Eliza, both holding back so many questions they wanted to ask her. But the sullen expression displayed by her reflection on the window was enough to keep even a hungry baby silent. Boa noticed her despair and mentally scrambled to find the words to say. Just as she opened her mouth to speak, Eliza beat her to the punch.

"So..." Eliza said, startling Boa as she snapped her gaze from Eliza back to the road.

"Yes?" Boa responded nervously.

"Gazi said your husband was a fugitive? From Japan?" Eliza questioned.

"Gazi?" Boa pondered to herself before chuckling. "Oh! You mean, Angel. Forgive me, Eliza. I've not heard that name in years. My family pretty much disowned me for marrying Hide. Angel is the only one who still communicates with me." Boa said in a light-hearted tone, completely unaffected by the devastating reality of what she just said.

"Your family disowned you for marrying your husband?"

Boa nodded just as she was pulling up to a red light. "Well. He is a fugitive after all. But they don't know him like I do. He may have a tough exterior. Very quiet and reserved. Sometimes he even scares me with his silence. But underneath it all he's the most caring considerate person I've ever met."

Thinking about her husband made Boa smirk. It wasn't too often that someone other than Gazi asked about him. Whilst parked at the red light, she took the opportunity to turn and give Eliza eye contact as she continued.

"It's hard to find a person, especially these days we're living in, who still has the ability to put themselves in another person's shoes and understand how you feel. Regardless of their relationship to you, everyone's in a rush. Everyone's in it for themselves, devaluing qualities such as politeness and chivalry. Yes, we're women. Equal to men by birth. But still. I'd like a man to hold open a door for me every now and then." She said before releasing a romantic sigh.

Eliza was beginning to warm up to her new maternal guardian. Her personality was completely unexpected in comparison to Gazi. It was uneasy and uncertain feeling that washed over. Can Eliza really coexist with such a positive being? Boa smiled and gave an instinctive nod just before the light turned green. With a gentle press of the acceleration, the vehicle continued on.

"I like your hair!" Rain said out of the blue.

Eliza turned to her and put on a wide exaggerated smile. "Thank you, Rain! And I like your name. It's so pretty."

Rain giggled to herself as Eliza turned back around.

"Get it? Their names?" Boa asked.

Eliza shook her head. "Um…Their names?"

"The oldest is Cloud, and the youngest is Rain. Because rain came after the cloud!" Boa said before bursting out in laughter, proud of her own joke. Her children also thought it hilarious. Eliza sighed with a smile. Such a peaceful family. She hoped her presence wouldn't turn out to be a burden.

Boa drove through the city to the northern most residential area of the Nowon district. It was on the outskirts of the busy metropolis, elevated on rolling hills to give a clear view of the impressively lit city skyline. The Shikagane residence was more like a manor, with a main house surrounded by a clay wall of Japanese design from the 1980s, suggesting that Boa's husband built it himself. The back of the house was facing the dense protected national forest that covered the Bukhansan Mountain with its smooth granite peaks. The towering pine and winding oak trees that swayed with the cool wind were the first features Eliza noticed when Boa pulled into the driveway. Trees were an unfamiliar sight to someone born and raised in one of the most technologically advanced cities in the world.

Coming through the front door, they entered the foyer. Rain and Cloud went through the usual procedure of hanging up their coats and taking off their shoes before running to their designated playroom. "Kids, dinner will be ready in one hour. Cloud share your toys!" Boa called out.

"Hai, hai, hai." Cloud uttered routinely.

Eliza just stood there, examining her new surroundings and wondering if she should follow suit and take off her coat and shoes. Boa found it hard to remove her grin. It was like bring home an adorable puppy for the first time. "Eliza, we hang our coats here. And leave our shoes here." Boa instructed.

Eliza nodded as she followed Boa's direction. Boa took the liberty of receiving Eliza's coat to hang it up herself. It was heavier than she expected, tough and durable. The green felt was smooth to the touch and the hood was full of strands of golden hair.

"This is a beautiful coat, Eliza." Boa complimented.

"Thank you. It used to belong to my mother." Eliza revealed.

"Oh." Boa responded, picking up on the tone that her mother must be either dead or missing.

"Your room's this way. I'll show you." Boa said as she pointed down the hallway.

The interior design of the four-bedroom house flaunted a welcoming atmosphere with warm earth colors. The dark brown stained wood flooring was well polished and without a scratch. Small porcelain Japanese figurines lined the numerous bookcases and shelves throughout the hallway. And the walls were a genealogical history lessons with thin digital monitors interchanging the photos of family members that dated back from before the last world war.

As they walked past the open living room, Eliza noticed several things. The living room itself was large enough to play a half court of basketball in. There was an ambiance of soft piano-driven inspirational Electronica music playing. This genre of music was always playing, as Boa had an irrational fear of silence. Behind the tan couch set was an array of polished Japanese weapons locked in a glass case that took up a whole wall. A flat screen TV monitor was implanted into the wall and in front of it, there was a large neatly rolled mat besides folded pants and a V-neck t-shirt.

"This is where I do most of my work." Boa told her.

"Are you a martial artist?" Eliza assumed.

"Mm-hmm." Boa said with a proud smile. "Ever heard of capoeira? I've been practicing since I was six. But it's more so meditational for me than an art of combat. You know? Like yoga. You have to isolate specific muscle tones with each move so that it eventually becomes muscle memory. I practice here. But I teach students out in the open plazas and market streets of Itaewon. It's a shopping district in the city. Pretty fascinating actually. I'll have to take you there sometime soon."

"What does your husband do?" Eliza asked.

Boa grinned nervously. "To be completely honest. I'm not sure. His cousins came from Japan to help him with his business. Some weeks he's a fisherman, bringing in a lot of money from the fresh catches. And then some weeks I see him wearing a sharp fancy suit and tie before heading out early in the morning." She said in a beaming smile.

Eliza looked at her like she was stupid. "That doesn't bother you?"

"Hmm… Not really. Why should it?" Boa said, still holding that blissful smile.

"What are those weapons for? You don't use those for capoeira do you?" Eliza asked.

Boa walked over to the glass casing and admired, specifically, the black mask that ninja wear when on a mission. "According to Hideo, they've belonged to the Shikagane family since even before the first world war over two hundred years ago. Oh! And I have to ask that you leave em' alone. Hide doesn't like anyone playing with them. Even I'm not allowed to dust them. *I'll dust them,* is what he tells me."

"Now then. Come along. You must be tired after flying for twenty plus hours right? Let's get you settled in." Boa said before continuing on with one of Eliza's suitcases.

Boa walked into Eliza's new bedroom. The orange security lights from the backyard penetrated the blinds, allowing Boa to locate the lamp on a nightstand and illuminate the room. The small bedroom was neatly furnished with a twin-sized bed, dresser, nightstand, and closet. Everything was colored some hue of green. Eliza entered and looked around. Everything was to her satisfaction, meaning there wasn't anything to complain about. With a deep sigh, she set her suitcase on the bed and unzipped it.

"I hope you like it. Angel said you liked green." Boa said with her fingers proudly clasped behind her lower back in self-admiration.

"Well, light vibrant green. Peridot. But this is good. Thank you." Eliza said as she took out a small 6x4 picture frame. The picture showed her hugging her father. It was taken a year ago on her last birthday.

Boa approached and examined the photo. "He has a funny smile."

"Yeah… He did." Eliza muttered. Boa felt the awkwardness as Eliza put the picture frame on the nightstand next to a digital alarm clock.

"Whelp. I guess I'll leave you to unpack and make yourself at home. I'll go and get dinner ready. Okay." Boa said before slowly backing out of the room.

"Thank you." Eliza let out softly as she sat down on the bed.

Boa smiled at her and leaned against the doorframe. "If you need anything at all, Eliza. Please don't hesitate to ask. Okay? We're your family now. Feel free to talk to me about anything." After receiving a nod from her new tenant, Boa left, closing the door and heading for the kitchen.

Eliza sat in silence, looking around her new room. She could hear the sounds of pots and pans clanging from the kitchen. After ten minutes passed with Eliza simply sitting there staring out into space, she finally moved her suitcase off the bed and lied down on her side. Her arms were folded and while she wasn't crying, tears ran down her cheeks as she stared at the photo of her father. Slowly…painfully… Eliza drifted to sleep, closing her watery eyes and hugging herself tightly.

In the middle of the night, all was quiet in the Shikagane house. The music in the living room was off. All of the lights were off, including in Eliza's room. She was still sleeping, only someone had taken the loving initiative to pull a blanket over her. And in the midst of her sleep, it appeared as if she reached over and grabbed the picture frame of her father because it was now in her arms.

Suddenly, Eliza's ears twitched. Her eyes slowly opened. In the dead of silence, Eliza could hear something. It was a sound that she was all too familiar with. A sound that dredged up a dark memory. A sound that was reminiscent of the night that she lost her father. At first she laid there wondering if she was just imagining things, but the sound was too consistent.

She looked at the alarm clock by her lamp. The time read 2:17am. Leaning over to turn on the lamp, she found a sticky note was attached to it. It read, "Sorry. :(I didn't want to wake you. There's a plate in the fridge. – Boa."

As Eliza sat up, her Furyx induced hearing honed in on the sound, making it much clearer and recognizable. It was the sound of a man grunting from a fight. Eliza put the letter down and got out of bed. She was still wearing her traveling clothes from the airport.

Opening her bedroom door, Eliza peaked down the hallway. With her vision, she didn't need any additional light aside from the soft orange security light that soaked through the curtains. Softly, she tiptoed down the hallway. As she past the foyer, she put on her shoes and grabbed her green jacket before continuing on. The sounds of grunts and aggressive footsteps led her into the living room and through the stone tiled kitchen. From the kitchen, there was a door that led toward the back patio. Eliza was certain that the sounds were coming from the back of the house.

Cautiously, she unlocked the back door and stepped out onto the burgundy colored wooden patio. A strong cold wind blew through the trees of the vast forest and made a rustling racket that sounded as if a storm was approaching even though there were clear skies. For Eliza, it was a beautiful sight to see the white moonlight glistening off the needle-like leaves of the placid pine trees.

The grunts continued. Eliza stayed close to the house walls whilst walking toward the side of the house. Just as she reached a corner of the exterior wall, she saw him from thirty yards out. A man dressed in a dark uniform like ninja was putting on an impressive demonstration of ninjitsu while using a short katana sword.

"Whoa." Eliza whispered as she lowered to squat with her back against the house.

The ninja moved and swung his sword with elegant grace and swift skill. Not a single movement seemed accidental or out of place. Everything flowed in a continuous fluid like motion. His sword was so fast. At one point, the sword was stretched out in front of him in a lunge. In the next, it would be flying by itself behind him before the ninja did a spin to reach out and catch. All of this happened in a smooth perpetual motion.

After two minutes of kinetic movement, the ninja stopped. A small gust of dust kicked up from his sudden halt. The ninja slowly turned and glowered at Eliza. He wore a black facemask just like the one that was in the living room display case. The mask only showed his dark slit eyes squinting at her with obvious disdain. Before Eliza could break her enchantment and realize she was being watched, the ninja threw two small metal ninja stars hurling towards her.

Eliza gasped at the shock of his sudden arm movement. And while she knew he threw something at her, what happened was even more stunning. Eliza watched the two ninja stars as they twirled towards her. Except for her, they were traveling through the air much slower than when he initially threw them. She couldn't believe it, nor did she have any idea of what was going on. Before her brain could register any of this, the two ninja stars flew just above her head and blasted into the side of the house with two hard metallic thuds.

Eliza fell back hard on her butt from squatting. Then she heard a distinct playful laughter. Looking up, she saw Cloud sitting Indian-style on the roof just above her. He was wearing the same black ninja outfit. His arms were wrapped tightly around his chest as he failed miserably to contain his amusement.

"She jumped!" Cloud uttered in Japanese amongst his glee.

"Cloud-chan. How many times have I told you not to make fun of those weaker than you? It lacks class." The ninja chastised in a low bass-heavy Japanese tone.

The man removed his mask to reveal himself to be none other than Hideo Shikagane. He was in his mid-thirties with rich dark black hair and a trimmed beard. He had the face of someone who hardly ever showed emotions. Like on his wedding day, the only expression he'd ever show was a grin that consisted of a slight raise of one corner of his lips.

Hideo extended his hand. Eliza reached out with one hand for Hideo to pull her up and the other hand to pat the dirt off the back of her pants.

"My name is Hide. My son, Cloud." Hideo told her. Eliza nodded, subconsciously adding a bow.

"Dad. She knows my name." Cloud said aloud before dropping down from the roof.

Dying to ask him over a million questions, Eliza waited till they were in the kitchen. Leaving the overhead lights off, Cloud set out a foldable kotatsu table for the center of the kitchen floor. The young child instructed Eliza as to where the shiki futons were so she could retrieve them as Hideo warmed up the meals Boa had earlier prepared.

Hideo, Cloud and Eliza sat around the table sharing bowls of rice, hot soup, and steamed well-seasoned fish. Cloud struggled to eat as he could hardly contain himself from giggling at Eliza. To the boy, Eliza was the funniest person he had ever met. It was so amusing to watch her fiddle with chop sticks and then open her mouth to eat a clump of rice, only to have that rice fall from the sticks before her nervously shaking lips could take it in. Truly like a puppy in a new environment.

After several tries, Eliza began to get annoyed with Cloud and could no longer hold back her natural squinty-eyed scowl of contempt. Hide chuckled to himself, which sounded like he was coughing. He gestured to his son to get up and fetch her a fork.

"Mr. Hide. What was that? That fighting style." Eliza asked him.

"You know martial arts?" Hide asked back.

"Well, I've always wanted to learn. All I know is what I've seen from my father. He did a little MMA." Eliza said as Cloud returned with a fork. Eliza smiled with an attitude-laced smile of gratitude toward the small boy. "I just watched him and copied whatever I saw." Eliza explained.

Hide nodded. "Hmm… Observation is the key to learning. Think of the originators and creators. It's not as if a book fell into their possession from the heavens. They watched and watched closely. And after watching a bit more, they created their own style, their own variation of the same concept. The art of fighting." Hide told her.

Hide patted Cloud on the head. His touch always seemed to incite a cheerful giggle from the small boy. "A child's mind is like a sponge, Eliza-chan. So is the mind of any true student." He told her.

Eliza pondered to herself. "But, how do you know who to watch?" She asked aloud.

Hide finally delivered his only grin for the evening. "If you want to be the best, seek out the best. Imitate them. And do what they did. Only do what they did, better." He told her.

Eliza nodded as she pondered at the notion. Hide may have thought he was just making small-talk. But in fact, he only lit the fuse to unlock a talent that Eliza had hidden away all along.

Chapter 5 – Self-Taught and Obsessed

Throughout her first few weeks in Korea, Eliza adjusted to Korean life in an unexpected manner. It didn't take her long to pick up the habit of walking the market streets after school. It was just fascinating how neighborly everyone was with each other. In Ybor, people were so enclosed in their own little bubble or clique. It was taboo to ask complete strangers how their day was or what was new with the family. But in Seoul, the venders knew their regulars and enthusiastically welcomed new customers as if they were welcoming a long lost son returning home. Unlike America, however, it was illegal to carry short ranged weapons. So it was rare to see people walking down the streets with swords, canes and nightsticks.

Sure she had troubles adjusting to the racial barrier and learning the different signs and street signals. But Eliza was never the type who just walked up to people and sparked up an innocent conversation anyway. Not to mention, while Korean was the national language, English was a necessary course to complete before graduation. Thankfully the music was just like the music she used to listen to, but with the spoken Korean language. A minor difference she not only tolerated, but appreciated.

During and after school, Eliza was always by herself with no friends and no one to talk to. Gazi didn't call her and she didn't expect him to. She did have a few friends in Tampa, but their personalities were just a mirrored reflection of her own. Eliza rarely called anyone to ask how they were holding up. So she didn't expect any of her Tampa friends to do so.

Initially, Eliza didn't dread the loneliness or fall into a depression because of it. In fact, she welcomed and preferred it. In Eliza's mind, she felt that she was truly the only one on earth who had lost her father in such a way. The saying, "someone out there has it worse or knows what you're going through," made Eliza sick to her stomach. Even if she did believe in that statement, it's not like the company of misery would comfort her. She didn't want to forgive or forget what happened. More so, she never believed that she'd ever forgive or forget.

Eliza soon picked up on the fact that Hideo was hardly ever home during the day. Since her first night in Korea, she wouldn't see him for another two weeks. When she did, he was only passing through on his way to or from work. Thankfully, she wasn't in a hurry to converse with him. Something about their talk of martial arts sparked a fire that couldn't be extinguished. And before she sought another philosophical conversation, she subconsciously felt that she needed to gain some experience under her belt. A foundation, so to speak.

Her new abilities with the Furyx Gene extended her limits with everything. In school, she only had to hear the teacher say something once and it was instantly committed to memory without the need of excessive studying. If she was showed how to do something, she need only see it once, and she would gradually imitate it to precise accuracy. At night, she'd wake up at or around three in the morning after sleeping for only four to five hours. It was all she needed. This left her to explore other avenues, like waiting on the back porch to possibly catch another rare sighting from Hideo in his ninja outfit.

On the first day of attending her new school, Eliza initially felt extreme alienation from her peers despite wearing the same uniform as all the other girls. She was the only white girl in the school. Sitting in the front of the classroom brought unwanted attention from both the boys and the girls. The hormone-enraged boys weren't subtle in their urges to check her out. Her smooth tan legs and naturally blond hair stood out amongst the colorful wild hairdos of the other females. The girls, staff members included, watched her in envy, silently joking to one another about how she seemed to resemble a sunflower that was poisoned. Eliza blocked them out, focusing on the teacher's instructions and trying her best to simply follow along.

That same very first day, during lunch period in the cafeteria, Eliza was unwrapping a packed lunch Boa made for her, still ignoring the jealous feminine glares that sat at the end of her table. In a designated corner of the room away from the tables and chairs, a group of five students were engaged in swordplay practice with wooden swords. This group of boys had to be in some kind of club because they were just a notch above amateurs. As she ate her lunch, Eliza paid close attention to the swordfighters.

The girls at the end of Eliza's table noticed how she went three consecutive minutes without blinking. Minzy, the leader of the pack, distinguished by her zebra striped sky-blue and black hair, finally had the courage to act on her disdain for the foreigner. Eliza didn't notice Minzy approaching. She just sat there spellbound, watching the swordfighters as if they teaching her a magic trick. As Minzy came closer, an astonished expression washed over her. She noticed that Eliza's eyes were almost fully contracted to the point that the black pupils were as tiny as a needlepoint.

"Yah!" Minzy shouted.

Eliza snapped out of her trance and glared at her. "What?" She barked back.

"What's wrong with you? Are you some kind of freak?" Minzy asked in near perfect American English dialect.

Eliza stood up and got in Minzy's face. Even though they were both freshmen, Eliza stood about four inches taller than her. "Yeah, I'm a freak. I'm a monster with long white fangs and I'm out of my mind. What are you going to about it? How does that make you feel?" Eliza growled.

Four more girls with heavy make up and colored hair slowly rose from their end of the table and strutted over to back Minzy up. Eliza scoffed with a smirk of excitement "You wanna go? Let's go." Eliza said as she raised her arms beckoning them to continue approaching. She was creating a spectacle of herself, a spectacle the other students surprisingly didn't find entertaining or pleasant.

Minzy was a good-looking girl who engaged in her share of catfights. But despite her youth, she knew fear when she saw it. And Eliza had no fear. Even if they did beat Eliza and drag her down the hallways it would do no good. Eliza would still remain defiant and never submit to her will. Not in a week. Not in a month. Not even till graduation.

"Nah, forget about her. She's just a loser. No guy is gonna wanna go out with her anyway. Too stuck up." Minzy told her friends in Korean.

"Hey! You know English! Say what you got to say, skank!" Eliza shouted.

Minzy shook her head with a satisfied grin and walked away. Her friends weren't as hasty as to let go of Eliza's insolence but reluctantly followed suit anyway. Eliza stood bewildered and frustrated. Why even try her if they weren't committed to make a move?

"Yeah! That's what I thought, you little rats. And I don't know what you call that hairstyle of yours but let me tell you, it's terribilarious!" Eliza shouted.

Eliza looked back at the swordfighters. The teens had stopped their practice to watch what was going on and by then, they had all cast judgmental looks upon the new student. Eliza rolled her eyes and threw her lunch in the trashcan. Then, she mumbled a couple of expletives to herself as she whipped up her book bag and headed for the exit. The whole cafeteria erupted in traumatizing laughter at the sight of her storming out.

That night, Eliza woke up for the first time at around two am. She tried to go back to sleep but ended up just lying there on her back, staring up at the ceiling for a couple hours more. First, she started daydreaming about Gavin from Ybor. She fantasized that, by chance, Gavin would follow her to Korea and befriend her while posing as a high school student. But after two hours of Gavin, the infuriating thoughts of Minzy and her classmates crept up. It was hopeless.

At around 4:30, Eliza sat up in bed, wide-awake and energized to start a brand new day. It was then that it had occurred to her that maybe she'd catch a glance of Hide if she waited for him to come home some time at night. In no time at all, Eliza threw on a green sweat suit, retrieved her shoes from the foyer and stationed herself on the back patio under the porch light. It was nearly freezing but Eliza prevailed. She just sat there watching the smoky peak of Bukhansan.

For hours, Eliza trembled in the cold until the sun came up. Rain was always up before her mother and would bundle up in a warm coat just to join Eliza on the patio. Rain's pure mind just assumed that Eliza was a fan of watching the sunrise come up over the city. Eliza would then take hold of Rain and sit her in her own lap, tightly wrapping her arms around the small child to keep her warm. For Boa preparing breakfast in the kitchen, it was always a comforting sight to see the pair in such tranquility. She wanted to paint them and keep the vision of them like that forever.

After her second day of school, Eliza walked the crowded downtown shopping streets of Itaewon in the Yongsan district. There were pedestrians everywhere and Eliza stuck out like a piece of charcoal on a field of snow. Boa was supposed to be giving a capoeira exhibition in an open public plaza and Eliza was hoping to run into her.

Instead, Eliza heard a commotion approaching. She turned around and accidentally dropped her books as a group of twelve older teenagers dressed in edgy street clothes ran past her. All of them bore the same intimidating glares of repressed anger and suppressed rage. They were carrying wooden bats and lead pipes while and rallying in chants of unified aggression. The spectacle reminded her of home and she couldn't fight the urge to explore.

With her hearing, Eliza was able to follow the gang from a distance without being so obvious. She didn't need to see which direction they took to know where they went. Carrying an armful of thick books, Eliza ran through the surprisingly clean alleyways and over fences to avoid suspicion. It wasn't until she heard the first fist-on-cheek impact that she picked up the pace and found the teenagers engaging in a massive street brawl. The battleground was taking place outside the loading bays of an industrial fabric manufacturing company, behind the building and away from public view.

Eliza crouched behind a dumpster and watched as the vicious battle raged on. It was intense with nearly thirty hot-blooded participants all between the ages of 17-20. Guys were getting hit against the head with lead pipes and thrown into brick walls. They didn't care about anyone living or dying. Dropping their opponents so they didn't get back up was the name of the game. She couldn't make out what anyone was saying, but had no doubts that the battle was a long time coming.

Suddenly, Eliza heard the loud vibrating sounds of an engine accelerating. Adding to the excitement, her jaw dropped as she turned around to see an electric motorcycle approaching at dangerous speeds. Matching the motorcycle's paint scheme, the rider was dressed in a red and white leather vented jacket and a dragon-designed red helmet. The rider drove directly into the midst of the brawl, slid it sideways and pushed off of the bike, slamming it into several rivals.

The shock factor gave the rider enough time to dust himself off. As everyone stood back gaping at the rider like he was crazy, the fearless daredevil took off his helmet. With his face revealed, an eruption of chants and cheers rang out as the rider tied up his long hair with a flare of edgy attitude and swagger. From the way he unzipped his jacket, Eliza concluded that this rider was a big shot whose presence would make a different in the fight.

After a brief pause, several gang members rushed the rider at once, all wielding some kind of weapon. Barehanded, the rider showed Eliza why they had good reasons to give him consideration. The impressionable blond foreigner watched as the rider swiftly gave a variety of devastating Tae Kwon Do kicks. He dodged and evaded their bats and pipes as if it were a break dance. Then he'd send them to the pavement with powerful lightning fast boots to the head and neck area. Needless to say, the charismatic rider was in a league of his own and Eliza studied him attentively.

That night, after waking up in the middle of darkness again, Eliza first went to check in Cloud's bedroom. She predicted that he would've been out practicing with his father, but was utterly disappointed to find him sprawled asleep over his bed sheets.

She waited a while to see if Cloud was just fooling her. Then she'd return to her own room, put on her green cotton sweat pants and jacket and make her way to the back patio with the hopes for a Hideo sighting. Only this time, she didn't just sit there waiting. What began as an experiment with her kicks to see if she could do it the same way as the motorcyclist earlier, turned into a full-blown Tae Kwon Do practice. She was out in the grass working up a vigorous sweat. Although she was horrible at first, she kept practicing till sun up before assuming her position on the porch in time to embrace the adorable little Rain. Eliza continued this routine for the rest of the week, each night getting better and better with the techniques.

On the Tuesday of her second week in the Nowon public school system, Eliza found a fortuitous treat thanks to her Furyx induced vision. It was during a gym period in the afternoon. The students wore white t-shirts and burgundy shorts as they participated in activities on the three-story school's rooftop. Most of the girls were playing volleyball on one part of the roof while the guys played half-court basketball on the other side.

Eliza sat by herself on the roof's ledge next to the chain link fence. While pretending to read her health book for credit, she caught sight of a building about 200 yards away in her direct line of sight. The building had a small hole about the size of a quarter in the top of one of its walls. Eliza grinned to herself as her pupils constricted to zoom in and watch a martial arts class in progress.

The Korean hapkido instructor stood in front of his class of middle-aged businessmen. They were all attending the lesson while on break from the nearest financial firm. The instructor was giving an impressive demonstration with the bo staff, a long slender wooden stick that was about five inches taller than the man holding it. He quickly twirled it around and showed a variety of aerial attacks, flipping in midair and swinging it about with superior control. It was as if the bo staff was just an extension of one of his limbs. The skill was called Bojutsu. Mastery of the bo (staff). Eliza laughed with glee as she watched, extremely grateful for her find.

For the next three weeks, Eliza mixed up her nightly routine of practice. For the first few hours, she'd continue the swift kicks of tae kwon do. And for the last foggy hours before sunrise, she'd use the handle of a broom to imitate the hapkido instructor's bojutsu moves, gradually getting better and better at it as if she was gifted with photographic reflexes. Each time she swung her fists or spun with a kick, or twirled the broomstick, the muscles in her body exhibited its own memory so that with each attempt, the movements became more natural, more fluid.

Practicing six hours a night, five nights a week paid off well. It was mental therapy more so than exercise and body conditioning. In the midst of her relentless practice, Eliza would lose sight of the hopeless emptiness she once felt. The hot-blooded pain of suppressed rage and anger would subside as she exhausted her muscles to their limit.

Not knowing how Boa would react to her new obsession, she hid it by taking up her capoeira classes after school. On the weekends, she would act as Boa's assistant in tutoring the elderly in the park. Eliza wanted to ask Boa if she knew that Cloud was practicing ninjitsu with his father. But she was concerned that it may lead Boa onto what she'd been doing just before the sun came up.

During conversations with Boa, Eliza kept her answers short and to the point. Even with the answers that required deep explanations, Eliza always gave it quickly, yet with a masking tone that was convincing enough to Boa that she was content with her new life in Korea. Boa tried her best not to ask questions about Eliza's past. And when she did, Boa would always go into what she thought was a funny story in her poor attempts to change the subject.

To Eliza, Boa was the most talkative person she had ever met. In the back of Eliza's mind, she wondered if she was always blabbering to suppress a dark negative feeling or memory. But Boa was just too perfect. She always seemed happy and cheerful, never raising her voice or even frowning, despite Cloud's penchant for mischief that she had to put up with on a daily basis. Thus, Eliza found Boa's personality painfully annoying because she doubted Boa's honesty. But so long as she was able to get her six hours of practice in, she was able to overcome her own contempt for even being in Korea.

After only three months of practice, Eliza was handling the broomstick exactly the way the hapkido instructor handled it. Only Eliza was twice as fast with her movements. Her tae kwon do kicks showed the skill of someone who has been practicing for a decade. After a while, Eliza had reached the point where she was beginning to get bored with her practicing. Everything seemed so easy and redundant. The suppressed anger and lack of fulfillment were beginning to seep through the cracks of her deception of peace. Her desire to meet with Hideo reached new heights and turned to frustration. She needed to learn more. She needed a new challenge.

During a lunch period one day, Eliza had her chin propped up by her hand while she watched the sword fighters practicing in the cafeteria with wooden kendo sticks. Even with them, Eliza was able to predict what each swordfighter would do next. This added with the fact that her vision greatly slowed down their movements, made the scene all too mundane and boring.

During gym class, while Eliza sat in her usual spot of the roof's ledge, as per usual she spied on the hapkido class. But even with the instructor, Eliza's patience was running thin. The instructor kept drilling the same techniques into his students over and over again. Or perhaps, it was that the bojutsu was the most interesting thing he displayed which made Eliza bored with him. Either way, Eliza slammed her book closed and buried her face down into her lap before letting out a loud grunt of frustration. Apathy was beginning to set in all over again. The few good things she loved about her new home had been played out. Now there was nothing.

On December 17, 2202, Eliza turned sixteen. It was her first birthday without her father. It was a tradition on her birthday that he'd always walk into her bedroom in the morning when the sun was in full bloom. Emil Christie would whip open the drapes of Eliza's windows, giving her a full dose of the orange glow. Eliza would then wake up on the spot, unable to hold back the laughter at her father's weird looking smile. Upon shouting happy birthday to his beautiful little girl, Emil would carry her out of bed and bring her downstairs where a birthday cake was lit on the table. Her presents were always neatly wrapped in green wrapping paper. Emil would always have a new outfit on hangers over a dining room chair. Every morning on her birthday…it was just Eliza and the father who cherished her.

At five in the morning, Eliza's tan face was glossy with sweat and tears. Her breath spewed visible in the icy cold air. She was practicing her own modified style of several martial arts. It was a mixture of tae kwon do, hapkido and the perpetual aerial movements that she learned from Boa's capoeira. She was pushing herself harder that morning than ever before. Each sweeping kick had more strength from the hips pushed into it. Each punch had more shoulder thrown into it. When she went to attempt her own variation of a flying sidekick, Eliza accidentally misjudged the strength in her quads and leaped nearly fifteen feet in the air before plummeting hard on the ground.

Stunned by what just happened, it didn't take Eliza long to figure out the Furyx gave her the ability to jump even higher than normal. Ignoring the freezing wet dew, Eliza just sat there in her burgundy school uniform skirt and looked down at her grass-scraped palms. They weren't bleeding, but she could feel the pain internally.

After staring at her palms in silence for little over a minute, a sorrowful pout set in as Eliza's eyes began to swell with tears. She shook her head no as if to tell herself that she wouldn't start crying again, but she couldn't help it. A lump of emotion formed in her throat as she bit on her bottom lip in anger. "Braden Pierce…" She uttered to herself as she continued to shake her head.

Pulling herself together, Eliza stood up with a brooding glare and brushed the wet grass off of her skirt. Staring at the forest, she wondered why after all that time, Hideo hadn't appeared again. She wondered if he was really so skilled to be able to watch her from the forest yet remain concealed from her senses.

It was still dark out, but Eliza sensed light approaching. She didn't feel like cleaning the sweat from herself and cuddling up with Rain to see the sunrise. She didn't feel like eating breakfast. She didn't feel like putting forth the effort to appear to be happy and satisfied. Before anyone else woke up, Eliza went inside and cleaned herself up. She changed out of her school uniform and into her casual street clothes of a thick white sweater top and some cotton size 8 khaki capris. After putting on one of her many silver bracelets and grabbing her green hooded overcoat, Eliza left the premises unannounced.

It was a cold yet serene morning with a soft overcast of clouds making way for the sun. Eliza skipped school and used the subway to travel down into the Gangnam district of downtown Seoul. The Gangnam district was one of the most developed areas in the city. Most of the electricity and light from the skyscrapers came from the Gangnam district. Eliza walked the streets listening to her mp3 player as she headed for the COEXtreme Convention center.

The huge ever-expanding four-story complex housed a mall, several hotels, a casino, an aquarium and the cinemas all under one roof. Everything was clean. Everything was updated with the most modern electronics and advanced technology. Eliza thought it was all superficial and excessive. Even though it was still morning, there was over 250,000 people roaming the massive halls and checking out the thousands of new inventions on display.

Eliza saw thousands of foreigners. But everyone was with someone or in some group. Everyone kept to themselves. Being around so many people made her feel even more isolated. Surrounded by so many yet still alone… Eliza couldn't stand it. She reneged on getting a bite to eat due to the long lines and it took her half an hour to exit the premises.

As she considered heading back to the subway station, Eliza traveled west on the walkway of Tehran Boulevard. The locals called it Teheranno. The massive eight-lane street ran through the heart of Seoul's version of Silicon Valley. Hundreds of architecturally ambitious skyscrapers were erected along the Teheranno. She had to shoulder her way through the mass of business men and women all talking in their native languages on cell phones or power walking to their next appointment. After five minutes of that, Eliza finally had enough and ducked in between a building alleyway.

Flattening her back to the building's cement wall to try and calm her nerves, Eliza was soon joined by a stray cat. The cat wasn't aware of Eliza at first. But as soon as it heard a sound from her, the tuxedo feline took off in a scurried rush.

Eliza rolled her eyes before looking back toward the sidewalks of the Teheranno. She couldn't stand the faces of those people. Those human beings… Everyone seemed to be in it for themselves. Everyone seemed to be in their own little world. All of it just pissed Eliza off to no end. She wondered if anyone randomly dropped from a sudden heart attack, would anyone care? She figured that they'd probably just step over the poor guy, telling themselves that the guy is alright and will be up shortly.

The deep strained exhale she let out through her nostrils did nothing to assuage the stress of joining back in with that crowd. It was a little past ten and she still had a whole day to fill before heading home. She sought adventure. Something significant that she'd remember on her future birthdays. She needed to do something that was just for herself. A challenge that only she as an individual could overcome and conquer.

Reluctantly stepping back onto the sidewalks of Teheranno, Eliza looked around at the different types of buildings towering over her. As if a beacon were calling out to her, her gaze gravitated back towards the COEXtreme center. It was there that she spotted her adventure. It was a dangerous and ridiculous thought. Even the most fearless daredevils would've come up with a better plan to accomplish it. But with Eliza being backed by her Furyx Gene, she honestly believed she could do it.

As she continued to navigate her way back down the crowded way she came, her ambitions grew from strong to adamant. She saw the building on her way to the COEXtreme center before but didn't consider it her own playhouse until now. Her eyes were set on Seoul's very own World Trade Center.

The 54-floor Trade Tower was one of the tallest buildings in Korea. The entire left and right face of the building was lined with one-way mirrors that reflected the images of its neighboring towers. While the backside of the building was completely vertical and nearly impossible to scale, the front facade was what interested Eliza. The frontal design of the building was dangerously steep, but shaped like a staircase with five monolithic tiers leading to the building's rooftop.

People were everywhere. It was nearly impossible to do what Eliza was planning to do without being noticed. But at that point, Eliza didn't care. As the brokers and accountants moved around her like a river stream around the rock, Eliza stood in front of the entrance looking up. The first leg of her trip was thirteen floors up before she could reach the top of one of the buildings massive tiers. The second tier would be another fifteen floors up. Then ten to the third. Ten to the fourth tier. And finally six floors to reach the top floor at a height of 748 feet into the sky.

With the acute vision of a hawk, she could see the edge of each window panel along the steep exterior facade leading up to the first tier. There was an only an inch and a half of space protruding from the window panes. Eliza would need to use the tips of her fingers to hold on the windows if she were to successfully scale the walls without falling.

After accessing the dangers to her health and the consequences surrounding the mystery of how she'd be able to achieve such a feat, Eliza took the ear buds of her mp3 player out of her ears and stuffed them into the pocket of her green overcoat. She loosened her legs by kicking them out and shrugged her shoulders aggressively to stretch out and warm up her rotator cuffs. An impulse burst of laughter was released as she firmly committed herself to the idea. There was no way she was going to let herself get caught.

Suddenly there was a loud blaring disturbance of screeching tires. Before anyone could look to see what was going on or about to happen, Eliza's ears had already discerned that a large moving truck was attempting to brake for a red light at a nearby intersection. The truck's collision with the driver of a dark van that jumped the gun on green was imminent. Eliza grinned as she lowered into a run-squat position. The echoing impact of metal and the screams and gasps that followed was Eliza's green flag.

While everyone turned to the horrific collision, Eliza sprinted as fast as she could toward the building entrance. With four quick steps, Eliza was able to scale an eighteen-foot wall and grab onto the lowest ledge of the inclined roof that covered the buildings lobby. With her Furyx-induced strength, Eliza pulled herself up like a world-class gymnast. Crawling onto the roof, Eliza wasted no time in bursting into another sprint, pushing herself to run as fast as she could. Completing her run on the slanted roof of the lobby was the most important part. She had to hurry because the lobby's ceiling was made of glass. If it weren't for that auto collision, anyone could easily look up and spot the jarring movements of what could be a terrorist or burglar.

With Eliza's speed, she cleared the lobby's inclined roof in less than four seconds. That's roughly faster than most football running backs running the forty-meter dash. Keeping in stride, she put it all on the line to jump from the roof of the lobby to the ridiculously steep wall of the main facade. Seven floors up at eighty-six feet above the cement pavement below, she managed to clamp her fingers onto the ledge of a window. She knew she couldn't stay in the same place for too long. Even if someone caught her hanging outside their window, if they saw her moving up, the employee would have a hard time explaining to their co-workers how a blond teenage girl could climb up so quickly and without a trace.

She kept moving. Not looking down. Not thinking about anything other than reaching for the sky. She'd switch between using the strength from her fingers and arms to pull herself up to the next floor like a jaguar climbing a tree. Or concentrating on the muscles in her thighs and quads to push herself running up the walls like an expert hill climber.

Once she reached the first steep tier, she kept going. She was still full of energy and didn't feel an ounce of pain or stress on her body. Even when she reached the second tier, she kept moving. The freezing air cooled her heated body and dried the sweat on her face. It was refreshing and exhilarating. Why stop? It wasn't until she reached the third high-rise tier at 598 feet up that she started to consider it may have been a bad idea to scale a skyscraper without any equipment.

She had only two tiers to go. There were only sixteen floors remaining to the top, but she stopped. With her hands on her knees and taking in strained breaths, Eliza turned looked out over the horizon. Her fingers felt like they were one keystroke away from breaking apart. Her burning triceps and back muscles felt like they were about to peel clean off of the bone.

The morning sun was still rising and with its altitude it seemed as if the sun was at Eliza's eye level. As if the sun came to keep her company. Her even tone seemed to glow in the sunlight. She couldn't hear anything but the cold breeze that blew through her now frizzled blonde locks. Looking down at the streets, the people were comparable to ants. Eliza felt satisfied and accomplished with making it that far. She thought, "Is the view from the top really that much better than it is here?"

Eliza cautiously stepped close to the edge of the ledge that was just above the thirty-eighth floor. Then, she slowly lowered herself to sit down with her legs dangling freely over the edge. It was a good time to take out her mp3 player, so she put the ear buds back in and started listening to music. One of the few things Eliza enjoyed about Korea other than martial arts was their DJs' penchant for mixing classical music with dance and metal. Thus, she found inspiration in Beethoven's "Moonlight Sonata" that was mixed with an eerie yet soothing metal guitar rift.

For hours she sat staring out at the sky with an emotionless expression, unaffected by the freezing breeze. Deep within her self-reflection, Eliza's thoughts kept slipping from the happy times she spent with her father to the night that he was murdered. She kept uttering Braden Pierce's name under her breath and she wasn't aware that she was doing it. It scalded her that she stayed pissed off brewing with hate for what Braden had done. While Braden probably had no idea she even existed.

Her thoughts dove deeper and deeper into the unexplained darkness. Her father was a respected detective. She knew other detectives in his precinct were on the syndicate's payroll. Everyone knew it. But who? If she saw Braden's face, why couldn't she take the stand to testify against him? Gazi already explained to her that a jury wouldn't believe that a traumatized fifteen-year-old girl could accurately identify the killer. And even though Gazi said that he truly believed her, to Eliza… that could never be enough.

She started to reflect on Gavin's words the night she was injected with the Furyx Gene. Her eyes squinted with spite as she remembered his voice speaking the following words in her head.

"Twas very foolish I think. About seventy percent of the gangs out there, on the streets and around the world are all under the shadow of their wings. They have political connections, entire law enforcement agencies on their payroll. They own banks, casinos, hotels. They are the arch prototype of what an organized crime family is supposed to be. Hence, that's why they're called a syndicate."

Eliza eyes glossed over and she felt the warm sting when her eyelids shut closed. When her eyelids opened, a small trail of tears ran down her cheeks. She ignored them and shook her head as if she wanted to call out the world for being cruel and unfair. She shouted, "Daddy! How can I bring you justice if the killer works for the most powerful group in the world? Even, with this strength, will it be enough? What can I…"

She stopped mid-sentence. She suddenly became aware of herself as if there were three more Eliza's standing up behind her. They were all watching her with a scowl of contempt. All displaying that signature ego-crippling attitude simply by their posture and body language with crossed arms or hands on the hip. And just like that. It was as if the three Eliza's had joined back in with the original and taken over. Eliza's sad pout and droopy eyebrows straightened up to show a deadpan look of unbreakable determination. She didn't blink. She didn't sniffle. She relaxed the muscles around her cheeks and eyes and breathed in deeply.

Then, with a wide-eyed grin, she let out a haughty scoff that came from the pit of her bosom. "Pssh! Doesn't matter. I'll kill him no matter what it takes. If anyone else wants some, then they can just form a line at the door. I'll slaughter you all. Fucking gangs. Pierce scum!"

…

The fulfilling sense of renewed purpose was Eliza's birthday present to herself.

...

With that firmly in mind, she gradually began her descent down the building. It was easier than on the way up. Wanting to test the limits of her strength, she intentionally dropped from the ledge, ten floors down to the second tier. It was terrifying and she knew she made a mistake the moment her toes left the edge of the roof. Although she was plummeting at a free fall, with her heightened sense of touch she had enough control and balance to straighten her body into a vertical position just before the moment of landing.

With surprise and shock, she planted on her heels with a bass heavy crack in the cement rooftop of the second tier. An echoing groan of stress and pain rippled out in the high altitude as the gravity slammed her chest down onto her knees. The impact knocked the wind out of her and she fell to her side with her arms wrapped around her breasts. Nothing was broken or dislocated, but she thought it best not try another jump like that again.

After catching her breath Eliza got back up and continued down, this time more cautiously. Floor by floor, she slid down the inclined walls of the building and dropped down to the pavement after reaching the lobby ceiling. Her sudden landing out of nowhere startled the bystanders. They looked up, wondering if she really came from the roof, but quickly dismissed the incredible thought.

"Sah rahm sal lyuh! Somebody call the police!"

Eliza knew enough Korean to make out the distress call as she looked over to her right. Nearly a mile, five blocks from her position, she could see eight grown men chasing a short, skinny male college student who was wearing a suit and tie. The eight men were dressed in blue and she recognized their white crab logo of a seafood restaurant nearby.

Eliza honed her vision to examine the college student. He looked like your typical spectacled scholar who's devoted his whole life to hitting the books and staying at the top of his class. Initially cynical and unaffected, Eliza saw the dread and misery pushing the wrinkles up on his forehead, the desperation that flowed through his sweat. The eight behind-the-counter seafood chefs were all big and burly. She had no idea what the college student did to piss those guys off, but did it really take eight of them? They were out to do harm and it was overkill. Unbecoming…

They ran into one of the side entrances of the COEX center near the aquarium and she wasn't the only one witnessing this. There were over a thousand witnesses, most of them adults in their middle ages. They were alarmed and apprehensive, but unwilling to take action. The most anyone did was called the police and report it in. Eliza's fists balled up as her hazel-tinted eyebrows descended over her green eyes. The whole little scenario seem distinctly reminiscent to a situation she experienced not too long ago.

"Fucking gangs." She grumbled in a steamy whisper.

The college student hit a dead end in the lobby of the COEX aquarium. Facing a blue wall-sized water tank full of tropical fish and coral reefs, the student gasped as he turned around to look for another path. There was an exit, but an elementary class field trip was in progress. At the moment, a mass of seven-year-old boys and girls stood in awe at the sweat soaked college student, wondering what the commotion was about. The young female staff members were about to approach him until they saw the eight men come barging in with a shouting fuss. The manager was at least wise enough to inform them that she was calling the police. But that didn't matter. The seafood workers cornered the young college student and began untucking meat cleavers from their aprons.

The college student dropped to his knees and kowtowed. "Please! I'm sorry. I'll pay you back as soon as I get my first paycheck. I just started my new job today." He wailed with sweat and tears glossing over his face.

"Oye! You said that last time. And you still haven't paid up!" One of the seafood workers shouted.

Just as the man approached and raised his cleaver, Eliza ran past him, jumped toward the glass fish tank and pushed off of it to ram the heel of her white tennis shoe square in the man's face. The force of her flying sidekick knocked the huge bulky man off of his feet onto the smooth marble floor.

Her speed left everyone dumbfounded. The most anyone saw was the golden flash of her blonde hair as she dashed amongst them. Even with the sight of their buddy folded up on the floor with his legs over his chest, they still couldn't comprehend what was going on. Eliza didn't give them a chance to figure it out. She wasn't there to introduce herself or teach some kind of moral lesson. Despite the fact that it seemed as if she was coming to the rescue, Eliza simply needed an outlet.

With ruthless aggression and an eye-squinting glare, Eliza leaped toward the seven remaining middle aged men with her fist cocked back. She completely let herself go without any regard to the consequences. Each kick she dished out with her Furyx-induced strength broke bones and ruptured organs. After a while, even the female staff members began to feel sorry and cringe from the hair-raising groans and screams of agony. The grown adults didn't have a chance. It was like a varsity high school football player bullying elementary students on the playground.

One of them finally got a clean swipe at Eliza, running the cleaver across the back of her neck. The man's eyes opened wide with terror and disbelief to find that there was no penetration. Not a single drop of blood was drawn. Only a red line emerging to show stressed blood vessels. Eliza simply turned around and punched the man in the mouth, dislocating his jaw and turning his four front teeth inward.

The sounds of whistles blowing from on-hand security guards were quickly approaching. Eliza had the last of them by his neck pinned against the wall. The man issued a strained apology but she wasn't in the mood for mercy. With a neck-breaking jerk, Eliza pulled him off the wall and spun on one leg to deliver high-velocity, pity-inducing back-heel kick to the side of his face. The man twirled as he fell face first on the cold marble, his eyes rolling to the back of his head.

The college student, staff members, bystanders and school children all stared at Eliza like she was a ghost from hell. She didn't care. With a nonchalant demeanor, she simply took off her green overcoat and fanned herself while strutting over to sit on a wooden bench in front of another water tank. A content smile curved upward from her lips. With a deep exhale of satisfaction she crossed her legs and stretched both arms out over the bench's shoulder rest.

She could have fled. It's not like anyone would've caught her. But there was something else keeping her there. Something she simply wanted to savor for as long as she could. Sitting on that bench in front of the tank of sea turtles, Eliza casually waited for security to come and take her away. Because the sight of eight full-grown bucks squirming on the ground, holding onto their body parts and straining to say their god's name in vain was yet another birthday gift to herself.

About the Author –

Revenge, Rivalry and Rebellion, Stage in the Sky is the theater that presents the entertaining stories and essays of neo-romanticist Rock Kitaro.

When I was fifteen, I read three books that would forever change my life. The most significant was Nancy Springer's "I am Mordred." If you know your Arthurian Legend then you know that Mordred is the name of the knight who kills King Arthur. But Nancy Springer's book told the story from Mordred's point of view. It told of his upbringing, his love, his ambitions.

It was amazing. Reading her book opened my eyes to the world of perspective. Before this, and even now, it seems so many people these days forget that there are two sides or more sides to every story. Even the worst villains are heroes to somebody else. No one just rolls out of bed with a desire to cause harm. And even if they do, there's a reason. So why not let the audience decide if that reason is good enough. This is what I do with my stories.

I'll go ahead and tell you that with my stories, I curse and can sometimes be choreographic with my fight scenes. Inspired by Lord Byron, all of my main characters are troubled individuals. They are sophisticated, arrogant, seductive, disrespectful of authority, self-destructive and struggle with a sense of integrity, what's right or wrong.

Make sure to visit www.stageinthesky.com for Rock Kitaro's latest releases.

The Three Kings of Ybor Saga –

Vol. 1 – Eliza Christie's Vendetta

Vol. 2 – The Wolves of the Syndicate

Vol. 3 – A Reunion of Beasts

Vol. 4 – August the 18th

Vol. 5 – The Kennedy St. Massacre

Vol. 6 – Beware of Romanticists

Vol. 7 – The Ides of March

www.ingramcontent.com/pod-product-compliance
Lightning Source LLC
Chambersburg PA
CBHW041729240626
47171CB00001B/2